Mirrors

Mirrors

Devjani Bodepudi

www.hhousebooks.com

Paperback ISBN: 978-1-910688-82-3
Cover design by Corah Hoeren and Creative Covers
Typeset by: Polgarus Studio

Published in the UK

Holland House Books
Holland House
47 Greenham Road
Newbury, Berkshire
RG14 7HY
United Kingdom

www.hhousebooks.com

To Baba,
Who believed I could

"Vakra-Tunndda Maha-Kaaya Surya-Kotti Samaprabha
Nirvighnam Kuru Me Deva Sarva-Kaaryessu Sarvadaa"

He sat with folded hands; eyes closed. The incense swirled around him in a thin wisp of fragrance. The temple was calm. The flowers: the frangipani blossom, like stars, the marigolds like sun drops and the roses, like ruby jewels, rested at the feet of the god with one tusk. He prayed for an auspicious beginning and a fitting end. He prayed for all obstacles to be removed and above all, he prayed for the fortitude to continue on the journey he had been chosen to undertake as a loving husband and a doting father.

He touched his forehead to the ground and thanked Lord Ganesh for the luck he had thus far shown him. He had everything he could possibly need and more than he should probably want. His daughter had been born today and she shone like the moon, iridescent and pale. She did not cry, she only smiled. He saw a fulfilling life ahead of her, of that of a beloved wife and a devoted mother. She would want for nothing except the chance to be reborn, to relive her happy existence again and again.

He walked back home, looking forward to seeing his two children, the boy and the girl. A perfect pair. The boy had big eyes, which seemed to challenge everything and curly hair, which refused to be tamed. They would have to shave it soon, as was custom but so far, his wife had not let them. He was already showing signs of being unruly, spoiled, demanding, always hungry. It made Amalendu Babu smile to think of the chaos the little one caused at home. The boy reminded him of himself. He would not be bullied, he knew, when he grew a little older.

The girl, they said, did not cry. Instead, she looked around her, inquisitive, intelligent. When he came to see her, he saw that she had grey eyes like his wife's uncle. They disturbed him slightly, reminding him of a ghost but the midwife said that sometimes this happened, and they would probably turn brown within a week. Amalendu Babu was appeased. He went straight to the sweet meat shop owned by his friend and bought a kilo of the sweet orange balls he loved so much. The ladoos were his favourite and were too troublesome for the women to make at home so it was the one sweet he would indulge himself to when the occasion arose. He had offered them at the little temple close to his home and sat facing the idol of Ganesh. His family deity was the Goddess, but it seemed fitting, today, the day of new beginnings to offer his prayers to the Elephant God first.

He had made the decision to travel England. It would take some time to save enough money from his father's allowance, but he would be able to do it. He might even be able to ask for an advance, telling his father he would send money home every month to pay it back and to contribute to the family. He was excited at the prospect of living like a sahib.

He thought about his wife and how she had been this time, during her pregnancy. He wondered whether she would let him sleep in her bed tonight. He would understand if she refused, she had just had a child after all. But he wanted to rush home to her today, nonetheless, to tell her about his decision.

PART ONE

Mothers

1

In the village where Mamta grew up she lived like a princess, she would tell her grandchildren. She had one servant to bathe her and one to brush her hair; one to dress her and one to feed her finger-mounds of rice and fish. She would swim in the pukur, larger than a pond but not quite a lake. It lay like a mirror just outside her house, still and clear, and when she looked into it she would see her twin, she would say. Occasionally, she would feel the tickle of the silver fins of the Roi and Catfish. Sometimes she would sit on the bank and watch the working women bathe and chat on the other side. They would look in her direction and giggle, suddenly making Mamta conscious of the differences between her and them. She could not hear what they said, but she knew they did not envy her. It was only many years later that she would understand why.

Mamta also liked to play with her brothers and sisters. She

was the oldest, the most responsible, and she excelled in playing mother to the horde of eleven children. Their own mother had no time for them – she had a household to run and in-laws to please and to serve. It was a matter of priorities.

Mamta remembered sitting on the porch with her youngest brother's head on her lap. It was the week before she was to be married. She was excited and impatient. She longed for her new life to begin and to fall in love, but her brother reminded her of the other feelings inside her, biting and clawing at her heart. She would be leaving her brothers, sisters, father, mother, uncles and aunts and grandmother, all for a new life, across the river.

"Will you come back, Bordi?

"Of course, I will, idiot!"

She slapped him on the head and then quickly kissed the spot.

"Baba is already sad. He keeps shouting at everyone when they ask him about the preparations."

"I know. But what can I do? They want me to be married, I want to be married, but that means that I have to leave, na?"

"Bordi?"

"Yes?"

"Is Jamaibabu your hero?"

With that, Mamta's brother pulled her hair, sprang up and ran away. She chased him, giggling, hitching her sari up to her knees, her hair coming undone.

Mamta smiled at the memory but with sadness at leaving her brothers and sisters behind. She looked at her husband now and wondered how she would tell him she was expecting their second child. She hoped he would have taken the hints and pieced together the evidence, but he was in his own world.

The man she married read voraciously. He would consume book after book as if they were tastiest rasagullas in the whole of Bengal. She had no idea what they were about, and he did not think it necessary to tell her. They had only the nights and stolen glances as she served him and the other men in the house their meals. Sometimes he would grab her waist and pull her behind a banyan tree as she walked to the tube-well to collect water for bathing. At other times he would call her on the pretext of asking to be served tea, then would suddenly bolt the door of the room where he was studying. But it was at night, when the lanterns were dimmed and only the glow worms and stars lit up the black nights, her husband would come inside her, without fail, whenever the time of month. So, when Mamta found herself with child in the first few months of their marriage, the women clucked and tutted. Surely it was too soon, they exclaimed. Perhaps she was with another man before marriage, just look at the way she lures the men of this house with her big eyes. She has no shame…

And now she was pregnant again. Her son was still a baby, her breasts still tender from the milk he demanded constantly. She was sure her husband would not be pleased. He used to disappear for days when she refused to share the bed with him at times during her first pregnancy. He would return, always in a better mood than when he left, but she could feel his rage every time he walked out of the front door. She dared not refuse him this time. Despite her fatigue at the end of the day, despite the fact that sometimes it hurt, Mamta lay back and let her husband take what he needed from her. She would then sleep as if she were a corpse, only to be woken by her infant son nuzzling at her breast.

The weeks progressed and Mamta's belly swelled faster this time. This time, there was no retching, there was no fatigue. The baby did not move as much as her first born and at first Mamta was worried

"Nothing to fear," said the Daima, the village midwife. "You're having a girl and in her own way she is strong. Her heart is beating like a drum and you are glowing this time. The last time, your boy gave you nothing but trouble and sapped your energy. Girls are not like that. They give. This one is here to protect you, she is giving you energy."

It was true, Mamta felt healthier than she ever had, but she could not let her husband share their bed even after she had resolved to do so early on during this pregnancy. She had grown brave enough to refuse him and again he left for days. It was of no matter to her though. For her, to feel this life inside her grow and blossom was enough.

The weeks turned into months and Mamta fell into a happy routine. The women in her household were praising her now, begging her to slow down, marvelling at her energy. But Mamta was content to cook and clean. These were tasks she was never taught in her father's house and earned her much derision at her husband's house when she first arrived, but now, it was Mamta who would take the lead in the kitchen.

During the final month of her second pregnancy, as Mamta was busy sweeping up the debris from cutting and chopping in the kitchen she suddenly felt the pain, the pull inside her telling her it was time. She was overcome with a drowsiness she had not experienced before. She managed to make it to her bedroom, and she fell on her bed, face first. The maid saw her and helped roll her onto her back, before calling Mamta's mother-in-law and father-in-law. Her husband could not be found, maybe he was at a Panchayat meeting across the fields, they said.

Within a few hours a baby girl was born. She coughed and spluttered life into her lungs and then gurgled and stared at her mother. Her brother, barely a year old, toddled into the bedroom, with only a black string tied around his waist to ward off evil and envious spirits and watched curiously as the women somehow managed to change the bedsheets around Mamta. She did not stir. Seeing that no one was giving him any attention, he screamed and screamed until the Daima picked him up, placed him on the bed and introduced him to his new sister. Mamta opened her eyes then. She was entranced by the girl child. They would call her Tara, after the goddess Durga and because she seemed to shine with a light of her own in the dark room.

Everyone agreed: she was the most beautiful child they

had ever seen. And as she grew, so did the love she brought into the world. Mamta felt bewildered that she could love her child so much.

Tara lived for only four years. In that time, Mamta recounted to her grandchildren, she would talk like an adult and behave as if she belonged to circle of matronly women rather than the gaggle of children who played every day outside their home. She would flummox her elders by questioning them on their ways and provide wise insights about the world around her. She would ask for paan, made from the heart shaped betel leaf, to be prepared for her after every meal.

One day, Tara saw a dead mynah bird lying at the foot of a banyan tree. She picked it up, curious at its stillness. The awkward rigidity fascinated her and so she brought it home. For a while, she played with the soft feathers, stroking them reverently. She marvelled at the tiny beak and claws and was sad that it would never sing and dance again. Tara wondered what she should do with it and remembered that all dead people needed a funeral. She would have to cremate it: no one else would.

She plucked flowers from the garden, filled a brass cup with rainwater, as she did not have access to holy water. Then she sat down in front of the bird, cross legged, palms together and eyes closed. From her lips poured forth the Sanskrit slokas she had heard her mother chant during her morning rituals, jumbled and incomplete, and for the whole morning she fasted as it seemed like the right thing to do. By the afternoon, Tara had gathered all the neighbourhood children and had instructed her brother to complete the cremation of the tiny creature.

Mamta was horrified and proud. She scolded the children for playing with the poor creature.

Tara replied, "It was all alone, Mama. There was no one to mourn it, not even its mother."

Mamta's reply was a tight slap to her daughter's cheek. Tara merely ran away smiling, looking behind at her mother. Mamta chased her, caught her, and held her close. She held her until she felt their souls had bound together so tightly that no one could tear them apart.

That night, Tara died in her sleep. She went as quietly as she had arrived and Mamta thought she could never love again.

2

The boy decided he needed to do something to help. He had seen his mother sad a million times, maybe more, but today she was crying. As she walked around the house, as she prepared breakfast, as she folded the clothes and put them away, Chotu could see her wiping her eyes. He could hear her sniffing. She was trying to hide it, but the tears were there, and her voice broke every time she spoke. Perhaps if he made her some tea she would feel better. He padded downstairs and headed for the kitchen.

He dragged a chair from the dining area to the sink and filled up the dented stovetop kettle with water for just one cup of tea. If his father was at home he would make him one first and then serve his mother secretly while his father was busy.

He placed the tea bag in a chipped china cup with flowers on the sides and measured out two teaspoons of sugar. On a

12

plate he placed two ginger-nut biscuits and took one for himself. As he munched, he hummed, briefly forgetting the sadness inside him.

"What are you doing, Chotu?" Shika, his eldest sister, asked as she walked into the kitchen. At fourteen years old, she was very thin but beautiful with long, straight hair. She wore kajal to make her already striking eyes bigger and rarely laughed, wanting to hide her crooked teeth.

"I'm making Ma some tea. She's sad today."

Shika frowned as she bent to take off her shoes.

"You'll burn yourself, Chotu, let me do it."

"But I've made tea a hundred and twelve times, exactly right," the little boy protested. He loved numbers and excelled at school now that he had finally come to terms with the language. Before that, he would stare blankly at the smooth white faces of his teachers and would wonder what their soft voices were asking of him. He imagined that this is what clouds would sound like if they talked.

Shika smiled wearily and pulled him in for a hug. She ignored the sound of the front door closing and hoped her little brother didn't hear. Chotu leaned into his sister and inhaled her perfume. She was the only one who ever had time to wrap their arms around him these days. Everyone else, it seemed, was content to either torture or ignore him.

"I know you have, little one, but why should you do it when I'm here?"

Suddenly, the kettle screamed. She shooed the boy outside and went back into the kitchen to read the letter she had

13

noticed lying on the sideboard. It was addressed to her in her mother's handwriting. As she read, she continued to make tea for nobody to drink.

Shika leaned against the kitchen counter and closed her eyes tight to stop any tears from falling; she let herself fall into the words of someone who now seemed a stranger. She lit the stove again and watched the edges of the paper curl and blacken. The flames spread, almost reaching her fingers as she refused to let the letter go until the very last second. Tiny fragments of paper ash floated in the heat, like miniature butterflies, grey, white and blue. She was at a cremation, but who had died? Her childhood, she thought; her mother, perhaps. She had to believe her mother would not come back, because if she held onto the possibility that she might, it would break her heart.

She wrapped her hair into a knot and finished making the tea. She called in her brother and watched and waited, knowing what was to come.

Chotu balanced the cup and saucer of biscuits on a stainless-steel thali, catching glimpses of his reflection in between the clattering, trembling utensils, all the way up to the bedroom. He knocked on his mother's door with his foot and shouted for her to open it.

No-one answered.

He called a couple of times and then left the tray outside her room. Perhaps she had fallen asleep, he thought.

Later that evening, Shika took out the milk pan to prepare Horlicks for her father and herself. Her mother would join them on most nights, usually a silent participant, almost invisible during this ritual. Shika poured the milk into the pan and set it on the stove, lit the gas with a match and watched the milk as it almost spilled over. Shika caught herself placing three cups on the counter and then cursed her own stupidity.

The resentment towards her mother for deserting her and her father for betraying her bubbled to the surface like the milk in the pan. Images of her father, sweaty and desperate with a faceless woman, images of Shika's sister, Tara, dying as her father panted and groaned invaded her and made her retch. She could not decide who she hated more. Tears came to her eyes and the smell of boiled milk was suddenly unbearable.

She poured it into two mugs, and took them to her father.

Her sister, Bella, was reading a Mills and Boon book on the bed they shared upstairs. Their two brothers were snoring in their bedroom. They had to be up at four to study; their father needed them to succeed. He was in the living room fiddling with the wiring of an old television set, distracted and content with his latest obsession. There was nothing here for her to do except look after Chotu. He was in his own bed now, but she knew that he would walk softly down the corridor in the middle of the night and squeeze into bed with her and Bella. Shika wanted to escape too, but there was nowhere to go.

Now there was a new truth about her father. Another sister, to replace the one who died. She was a secret, a stain, and Shika wanted to make things clean. She looked around the cluttered

15

room with the yellow light, the brown armchairs, and creeping tentacled spider plants her mother had nurtured.

Her father walked in and sat down in an identical armchair to Shika's. He looked at his daughter and quickly turned away. She looked like his own sister, light skinned, with crooked teeth; but Shika had his wife's temperament. In spite of this, he doted on her, she was his little pori or fairy.

When Amalendu Kumar Chatterjee found out that his wife had left, some part of him sighed with relief. Another part wanted to tear the house down in rage, and another wanted to weep. His wife was his anchor. He had made mistakes and yes, he had treated her badly, but he had loved her from the very first moment he saw her in her own father's house, playing with a childish doll, wearing a sari which could not hide her curves. It was a mistake to tell her the truth, he realised, about the money she had noticed go missing every month. He wondered how much Shika knew.

"Baba, I'm going to bed."

Shika startled him into spilling some milk on the cotton lungi he wore in the evenings. She moved quickly to fetch a cloth, wiped away the milk, and washed her hands.

"Yes. Beti, you need to get some rest. You've been working very hard. Listen, tomorrow, there will be no need to cook. I will cook tomorrow."

"But Baba, you can't cook. It's OK, really. I'll manage with Bella's help."

"I can cook – Just you wait and see."

As she climbed the stairs, Amalendu felt the distance between his favourite daughter and himself and he finally understood the enormity of what he had done.

"Fuldi, does Ma love me?"

"Yes, you're her favourite."

"Then why did she leave us?"

"She was unhappy here."

"Because of us?"

"No, because of Baba."

"I hate him!"

He spat the words out, as if they were a curse. He hugged his sister closer, pressing his cheek into her back, feeling the bones in her spine reassuringly hard against his face. Bella Didi had just climbed back in through the window. He cursed her too. He was full of anger tonight. He would be squashed now, in between them both.

Bella threw him a Marathon bar and shimmied out of the too-short dress. She wordlessly put on her pyjamas, removing her bra like a magician.

Chotu watched, sprinkling chocolate crumbs all over the bed as he ate. He was sitting up now.

"Where did you go, Bella Didi?" Chotu asked.

"I went to the cinema. I watched a movie with my friends."

"Did it have Mithun in it?"

"I watched an English movie, idiot."

17

Shika tried to ignore them both, burying the anger she was feeling against her sister as deep as she could. Sometimes she wished Bella would just run away like she had kept threatening to do. At other times she worried about her – she did not trust her friends and knew she had a boyfriend. And she worried what her father would do, if he found out about her secret rebellion.

"I have some news."

Shika did not move, pretending to be asleep. Bella shook her until Shika relented. She threw the covers off herself and sat up.

"I'm getting married."

Shika resisted the urge to laugh in her face. She closed her eyes and breathed deeply. "You're thirteen years old. Who are you planning to marry?" Her voice remained steady.

Bella crossed her arms. "I'm marrying Mickey from the Wing Wah. He proposed, and I accepted."

"But Mickey's not your boyfriend and he's only fourteen. It's against the law."

"It doesn't matter. Rishi has no style and just hangs around the bike sheds smoking. Mickey writes me poems and says he loves me."

"It's still against the law."

"We'll run away to Gretna Green and pretend we're sixteen. We're leaving next Saturday."

"I'm not sure it works like that, Bella." Shika kept her face poker straight. She was playing a game with herself, challenging herself not to laugh. Chotu's face, too, was serious. But he was not pretending.

"Well, I think this family has enough of perfect, don't you? Tara, so perfect, and then there's you; so perfect you have to pretend to be Ma! I will do whatever I want and you're not going to stop me. You couldn't stop Ma from leaving, could you?"

Bella's face was red, her fists were clenched. Shika felt the blow and looked away. Tears fell but they didn't see. She wiped them away.

"But I don't want you to go, Bella Didi," Chotu said.

Bella collapsed on the bed, as if defeated. Her face was suddenly buried in her pillow, her shoulders shaking. Shika stroked her sister's back and hair, trying to smooth away the hurt.

"I don't think Bella is leaving, Chotu. Not yet, anyway."

"Why not?"

"Because she would miss us too much and this isn't her time to go."

Bella said nothing. She only cried until she fell asleep on her side of the bed. Chotu and Shika lay down in their usual places; Chotu in the middle, making sure his toes were touching some part of Bella, while he wrapped his arm around Shika's waist, burying his face in her back.

Mamta returned home to the grey Birmingham terrace a few days before Shika's eighteenth birthday. Shika did not know that there had been letters back and forth between her parents for the four years of her mother's absence. It appeared as if all had been forgiven but it was Shika who remained the mother. As she grew older, she vowed that she would not become the woman she saw her mother was. Her choices would be her own.

By the time Shika had chosen to marry the white man she knew her parents would not approve of she had made peace with the darkness lurking like a silent demon inside her. The man she was to marry had also made his peace with that, believing he could see past it into a light beyond.

Their wedding, when finally approved of, was held in Kolkata, just as Shika's parents had wished. Both mother and father were present. No expense had been spared and, to the world, the scandal of a runaway wife never happened. As she took her own vows, with Agni, the fire god as their witness, Shika wondered at the truth of it all, the point of it all.

3

1992, Winter. Nuneaton, England.

Six-thirty in the morning and still dark. It would remain that way until eight and then the sun would rise in the grey sky. Shika's lids were heavy and she closed her eyes again. Ten minutes later, her husband shook her awake. She grunted something which he understood to mean that it was up to him today to get their daughter ready this morning.

Shika moved through a haze, especially in the winter months. Her unwillingness to get out of bed and dressed on some days meant that her daughter often found herself without her mother. On other days she would scream and throw things at her husband for the most trivial reasons – forgetting to buy sugar from the grocery store, failing to switch the bathroom lights off, not taking out the dustbin. Sometimes her tears would fall relentlessly.

In the summer, she was better. She baked cakes, looked

for work, socialised, cleaned and occasionally drank until she was merry. Everyone liked that Shika.

Chotu was seventeen when Shika married and he would regularly turn up at her doorstep after school to do his coursework, to watch a movie, simply to escape the boredom and beatings at home. He idolised his brother-in-law and doted on his sister; during Shika's pregnancy he would stay to help with the housework and make her laugh during the times when her husband could only watch in concern as she slipped into melancholy. More than ten years later Chotu, usually unemployed or finding temporary casual work was somehow little changed, and he still found in their home a refuge.

On this morning, before the sun had risen, Chotu was asleep on the sofa. Tara, Shika's twelve-year old, dressed in her school uniform, switched on the kettle, placed three mugs out on a tray with tea bags and sugar, then put some milk in the saucepan to boil for her cereal. She longed for cornflakes with ice cold milk just as she had seen on television but Shika insisted that she have hot milk with Weetabix: flavourless biscuits of dried wheat that turned to mush. Chotu still loved it, but it made Tara gag. She had tried rebelling, but her mother was too strong and too fierce to ignore. Some days, like today, Tara would make her breakfast, dilute it down with water and pour it down the sink, to make it look like she had eaten it, leaving the unwashed bowl in the sink.

Somewhere in the neighbourhood glass hit the pavement and shattered, a baby wailed, and Jeremy, their neighbour's dog, yapped as he always did at this time of the morning.

The cramped familiarity of the two-bedroomed former council house comforted Tara. The sound of her uncle snoring and her father's footsteps as he entered her bedroom to open the curtains added up to a happiness. To her parents, she was a blessing.

Tara made the tea and placed it on the dining table, which was in the same room as her uncle and the sofa. She removed the quilt from the sleeping man who was deep in his dreams then bounded up the stairs, calling for her father, who was still in the bathroom. She supposed her uncle would wake soon enough now. Her father, with his brown hair and blue eyes kissed her lightly on her forehead as she greeted him with a head butt in his stomach. Tara was tall, but her father was almost a giant. He towered over all of them. He always seemed to look like he did not fit into their little brown family. But no one really fitted. Tara looked nothing like her mother or father and yet, her father was like the glue that held them precariously all together.

From her bedroom upstairs, Shika could hear Tara. She did not stir. She waited until the house was quiet and then went quietly downstairs.

Her husband had taken Tara to the private school, in an area Shika had only driven through. She placed the cold cup of tea in the microwave and sent a silent prayer up for her daughter. She resolved to make tomorrow better. She would apologise to them all this evening, she decided, and set about gathering the ingredients together for a chocolate cake.

Chotu still slept.

4

Those days were in the past. Years had gone by without Shika needing to escape the way needed to then. She believed she was stronger now.

Shika brought home the dried fish from the Bangladeshi fish mongers, close to her parent's home. She unwrapped it, letting its pungent odour exude through its dead pores. The smell would linger for hours, if not days and her husband would complain for days after that. But it was for Bella, so he would not make too much of a fuss.

She roasted the dry fish for a minute or two to remove the sand and then let it soak in some saltwater. She then sautéed some sliced onions, ginger and garlic in some mustard oil before adding the spices and chopped pumpkin and potatoes. She placed the lid on the wok and cursed when she spotted the dent that must have been made by her husband. She let it go and let the vegetables cook for a short

24

time while she cut the fish into pieces. She added the fish and stirred lightly, making sure that all the ingredients were well coated with the spicy gravy that had now formed. Once cooked, Shika boiled some plain white rice and packed everything tightly into a Tupperware box. She wrapped the box in two plastic carrier bags, to prevent the smell from emanating any further She washed her hands several times to try and remove the smell from her skin. She scrubbed her fingernails and applied a hand cream but was still aware of the lingering stench of dried fish on her fingers and her hair. But it was for Bella.

Shika pulled up at the hospital and drove around for some time before she found a spot she could comfortably park in. She took the parking ticket and went back to her car to display it in her window. She carried the food in her handbag and wondered if anyone suspected what it was that she was carrying. She told herself she didn't care, but a part of her did not like to break any rules, even though the nurses had said, in Bella's case, it would be fine.

Bella had been given drugs that made her retch, chemicals pumped into her to kill the cells that were killing her, but it seemed only to make things worse. She had lost weight because she could not eat but this morning she made her husband phone Shika and tell her she wanted some Shutki: dried fish curry with some plain white rice.

It was lunchtime when Shika arrived. Bella was asleep. Her lips were surprisingly pink and glossy from the Vaseline she applied constantly, always aware of the painful dryness she was experiencing everywhere else. Her cheeks were hollow and her hair, although had grown back, was thinning again. She opened her eyes when Shika walked in but closed them again quickly. Her husband, a tall West Indian man, sat small, hunched and defeated on the other side of the bed. He did not get up. His eyes were soft, when so often she had seen them laughing, hard or mocking. Today, they held a little gratitude mixed in with the pain.

"Go and have a cup of coffee. Stretch your legs. I'll stay." Her tone was authoritative. She sounded like she was in control.

He obeyed but could not stay away for long. Shika was still wearing her coat and holding her bag when Bella's husband returned. His sister-in-law's hand covered her mouth, stifling her sobs as tears fell unheeded from her eyes. Bella's husband found another chair for Shika and asked her to sit down. She couldn't sit for long. She rose, left the food on top of the little bedside cabinet and walked out of the hospital room just as her sister's eyes searched her out, hoarsely whispering for her as she left.

Two weeks after that, Bella died. Shika was there with her. That time, she made sure she held her hand, whilst Tara and her father sat outside in the waiting area. Shika made sure she watched and listened to Bella talk in her sleep. She made sure she fetched the coffees and food for Bella's husband and teenage son. She made sure she was there to fluff the pillows and to rub salve on her sister's hands and feet, but she could not forget her cowardice that one time her sister looked for her.

PART TWO

Wives

5

Akanksha – 1980. Calcutta, India

"Oh, you who feeds life-sustaining food, nourish my visitors, friends, parents and offspring with food and drinks. I as a form of Vishnu, take this first step with you for food."

"And I with you, my love."

"Oh, thoughtful and beautiful lady, with a well-managed home, with purity of behaviour and thought, you will enable us to be strong, energetic and happy. Oh, beautiful lady, I as Vishnu take this second step with you for the strength of body, character and being."

"And I with you, my love."

"Oh, skilful and beautiful lady, I promise to devote myself to earning a livelihood by fair means, to discuss, and let you manage and preserve our wealth. Oh, dear lady, I as Vishnu cover this third step with you to thus prosper in our wealth."

"And I with you, my love."

"Oh, dear lady, I promise to trust your decisions about

the household and your choices; I promise to dedicate myself to help our community prosper, the matters outside the house. This shall bring us respect. Oh, my lady, I as Vishnu take this fourth step with you to participate in our world."

"And I with you, my love."

"Oh, lady of skill and pure thoughts, I promise to consult with you and engage you in the keep of our cows, our agriculture and our source of income; I promise to contribute to our country. It shall win us future. I as Vishnu, take this fifth step with you to together grow our farms and cattle."

"And I, with you, my love."

"Oh, lovely lady, I seek you and only you, to love, to have children, to raise a family, to experience all the seasons of life. I as Vishnu, take this sixth step with you to experience every season of life.

"Feeling one with you, with your consent, I will be the means of your enjoyment of all the senses. Through life's seasons, I will cherish you in my heart. I will worship you and seek to complete you."

"Oh friends, allow us to cover the seventh step together, this promise, our Saptapad-friendship. Please be my constant companion."

"Yes, today I gained you, I secured the highest kind of friendship with you. I will remember the vows we just took and adore you forever sincerely with all my heart."

The seven vows taken during a Hindu wedding ceremony, the seven steps of life...

"You're losing weight, Ma," her father-in-law tutted.

"No, Baba, I'm fine. I'm dieting a little and walking much more. I'm trying to be healthy."

"You have dark circles under your eyes. I think you're missing our Tinku!"

"Yes, Baba. Please drink your tea, it's getting cold." Her response was sharper than she had intended. She bit her lip and continued to pick the dirty clothes off the floor.

The old man chuckled. He saw his daughter-in-law was getting flustered, so he tried to concentrate on the paper. She was a good girl, he thought. She had come into their home five years ago and it had been a pleasant, peaceful time. His son was away on business for three weeks in a month and it was good to have Akanksha around to talk to. He really was very lucky. There was only one desire: Tinku really needed to be home more.

Akanksha pulled the sheets tight as she folded them under the mattress. She fluffed the pillows and smoothed the cotton bedclothes. Pulling the end of her sari into her waist she set about dusting the dresser crammed with her mother-in-law's perfume bottles, elixirs and hair tonics. She moved the pot of powdered vermillion and some of the red powder fell onto the dresser top and onto her clothes. It was troublesome to remove, this stain of sindoor.

She left the room and walked to the kitchen. Yawning, she pulled out a tin of biscuits from the top cupboard, picked up the tea that her mother-in-law had made for her and sat on the floor with her back against the wall. The scavenger mynah birds chirped outside the open window, waiting for scraps. Akanksha ignored and looked around. The cupboards should be replaced, and walls needed repainting. Everything seemed grimy. Her tea was cold; she sipped it, nonetheless.

"Cha khachish, Bouma? Tui Kha! Drinking your, tea? Please carry on." A deep rasping voice came through the kitchen doorway. Her mother-in-law entered the kitchen followed by a young maid carrying two bulging jute bags of vegetables. Akanksha continued sipping. The maid began sorting the various leaves and produce as the older woman set a saucepan of water to boil for some tea for herself and the maid. It always helped to look after the staff, she believed.

When Akanksha first arrived as a new bride, she would rush to the kitchen to help. Soon her mother-in-law assigned her other duties and practically banned her from entering the room, which was so full of dangers for a young woman.

"We can't have you burning yourself, now can we?" or "What would happen if you cut your finger?" and "You should smell of rose petals, not fried onions!". "What will Tinku say when he comes home?"

Akanksha remembered her wedding night, the fumbling, the forced weight upon her chest, the smell of alcohol on his breath. She remembered feeling nauseous at thought of this stranger touching her skin. But like a good daughter, daughter-in-law, and wife, she obeyed. She did as she was told. How could she not?

After a few months, she saw her husband less and less. He was away on business, he said. He made no apology nor sign of any desire to return. Akanksha was relieved, but what was her place now? Her mother-in-law delivered a verdict.

"There is a woman I know, she will come and see you next month. In the meantime, you must look after yourself. You must sleep more, eat more, work less. This will be for the good of everyone, you'll see. You'll thank me."

From that day, Akanksha stopped trying to help in the kitchen. She would have her morning tea that her mother-in-law made for her, then she would spend some time with her father-in-law, playing Karoms and discussing the news. Later she would leave to be waxed, preened and to have facials and hair spas. It was her duty now to always look presentable. For now she had a role; a kind of purpose given by the woman Mrs Majumdar had brought to her.

Today was a facial day. After her tea, Akanksha got ready. She wound her long hair into a bun and held it there with pins and bands. She longed for it to be cut short like the American actresses, perhaps even shorter, like a boy, but she knew it would never happen. A woman's beauty was her hair, her mother always told her.

She left the house without looking back and wondered for a moment, as she did every day, whether she should bother coming back. She knew she would.

She passed the cow grazing quietly on the side of the road, she waved to Mrs Sen, who was getting into her car, and finally she arrived at Dolly's Beauty Parlour. Inside was a tiny, shiny room, with wash basins, large mirrors on the wall and a range of expensive cosmetics on display. Akanksha was greeted by a petite Nepalese woman dressed in black, with hair sleek and short, who was ready to thread anything, anywhere. She seated her client and stroked her forehead.

"Just the usual for a Tuesday?"

"Yes, please."

"You'll need a hair spa next week. You're so lucky your mother-in-law allows you to spend so much time here. Not that I'm complaining!" She giggled at her own joke, hoping to make her client smile.

"Yes, I suppose so."

Akanksha lay back on a couch and let the tiny pricks of pain melt into her. She listened to the rhythmic friction of thread on thread and for a few moments she forgot who she was.

Meena watched her client every time she came in. She worried about her, no matter what the outcome, her client's smile seemed painted on, never quite fitting with the expression in her eyes. It was a gesture of thanks, but not of gratitude. Other women beamed and looked constantly in the mirror, during and after the whole session; Akanksha hardly glanced at her reflection. Meena took out the pestle and mortar, added some fresh fruit and other ingredients already prepared by her assistant and resumed pounding. She counted the times the stone hit stone and when there was nothing but a smooth paste, she relented. This was her speciality. She glanced at her client again and noticed a tear trickle slowly down her face, but it was wiped away quickly.

Meena scrubbed, patted and massaged Akanksha's face

with various different masks until at last she finished with one smelling of mints that tingled on her skin. She smoothed it deftly onto her client's face to reduce the wrinkles and blemishes. Akanksha gave in to the process. There was nothing else to do.

Suparna Roy's husband told her that he was having an affair, and she retaliated by telling him his son, in fact, was not his. Vikas Roy knocked over a vase in rage and went to strangle his wife with one hand as he pinned her up against the wall next to a painting of Tagore. Just then, the doorbell rang. Mrs Majumdar cursed. The characters all froze as she pressed the pause button on the VCR remote.

Akanksha stood at the door, her eyes cast down. Mrs Majumdar was irritated that she had forgotten her key and told her so, with a click of the tongue and a shake of the head. But all was soon forgotten as her daughter-in-law handed over a large bundle of cash from the day's earnings.

"You are a good girl, Akanksha. You are doing what your husband should have been doing. We are blessed to have you in this family. Now go and bathe, wash all that make-up off and change your clothes. It would not do for your father-in-law to see you like this."

It was the same every time, Akanksha thought in annoyance. Surely her mother-in-law need not remind her of the obvious every time she walked through the door. However, Akanksha saw it for what it was. It was a basic need to show her she was still in charge. She gave the orders around here and people must follow them.

Akanksha complied and went to her room on the first floor. It smelled faintly of Good Knight mosquito repellent and moth balls. Soon these smells and the smell of bleach would mingle and merge with the scents from her shower, as the maids entered to sweep and mop the floor for the second time that day.

The sun cast the orange glow of late afternoon. Her bed was neatly made and Akanksha felt it calling to her, seducing her with the promise of softness and sleep. She had a few hours before her father-in-law would expect to see her pottering around the house and bringing him his evening tea. She must hurry if she wanted that nap. Akanksha lay down on her bed. The whir of the fan and the voices from the television coming from the floor below lulled her into a deep sleep. Akanksha dreamt of brothers and sisters and father, but when she woke up she could remember nothing except the feelings of loneliness and loss.

It was dark. She had slept too long and now had to rush to see her father-in-law. He liked to discuss his day with her and talk about politics or cinema. Sometimes when Tinku had some free time Mr Majumdar would suggest that they all go and watch the latest Bengali release. She would agree enthusiastically and smile broadly, there should be no greater pleasure than an evening out with her family. Inwardly she pitied the old man with his eyes veiled grey with cataracts and his simple dreams.

6

Saira – 1978. Calcutta, India

Tinku was virtually invisible at work. He worked diligently and prided himself on his punctuality, but he had no friends because he didn't really know how to talk to them in the English they used, and Bengali was frowned upon in the office. He did, however, have drinking buddies. His friends from college would meet him after work and drink themselves into a stupor, eventually staggering home to their families. A few of them kept mistresses, if they had the means. It was quite acceptable.

The day Tinku met his mistress was during his second week at work at work. The receptionist had also started on the same day and they were drawn to each other immediately he remembered. She was thin, like a reed and her skin was dark and luminous, like the Goddess. Not many people would call her pretty, but everyone called her striking. Her eyes flashed either in annoyance or amusement and although she was young, she quickly proved herself to be efficient and intelligent. Within her first month there, it was common knowledge that she knew what she wanted and would do wondrous and unspeakable things to get it. With her large mouth and full lips, she seemed to hold the promise of so much pleasure behind the locked door of the stationary cupboard. Tinku believed himself to be in love and knew he had to possess her: he wooed her with pearls from Hyderabad and silks from Benares; he recited poetry in her ear whilst in the elevator to the canteen and lightly flicked his tongue on the lobes that held gold studs from his mother's jewellery box – she did not flinch, her eyes looked ahead, and her lips parted, just a little.

One day, he followed her into the ladies' washroom and locked the door. His heart was pounding. He would confess his love to her, marry her and she would be his queen. Saira stepped out of the toilet cubicle, barely glancing in his direction. She washed her hands and watched him in the mirror as he shifted his weight from one foot to the other, mumbling something.

"What do you want?" she asked curtly.

"I want you. I want to marry you. I love you, Saira."

"And this is how you propose, is it? In the washroom?"

"I needed to be alone with you."

"Hmm… What you really want is to fuck me. You all do. But you can't afford me, Tarun."

"I'll give you everything you want. I'll make all your dreams come true. I've seen the way you look at me and I know you want me too."

"I refuse to be just a wife with a husband to feed and a mother-in-law to fatten. I'm not going to clean your house and I certainly won't be having any ghastly babies." She turned to face him. "Do you still want me?" She unfastened her top button. Her collar bones jutted out of the V of her shirt. "Well, Tarun? Do you?" She undid another button and stepped closer.

Tinku gulped.

Saira lifted her top up and over her head and threw it on the floor. She was a breath away from Tarun now. The lacy fabric of her bra brushed against his shirt. She could feel his erection and smiled. She loved how she could do that. She slowly undid his belt. Tarun blushed. He wanted her badly now, but she was taking too long. He cupped her left breast and lifted the bra out of the way. For a few moments he just stared as she stroked his hair, but then he bent down and tasted the tip of her almost black nipple, savouring the salty sweet spring against his pink tongue.

He licked and sucked and then, with a whimper, he came. "Oh dear."

Saira quickly adjusted her clothing and fixed her hair. She walked out of the washroom, without so much as a backward look – leaving Tinku even more certain Saira would be his at whatever cost.

A few intimate meetings later in various rooms of their workplace, Tinku and Saira had made an arrangement. Saira would live in a flat in Ballygunge, overlooking the Birla Shiv Temple, and Tinku would spend his nights with her. She would agree to be exclusively his so long as he kept her happy. Essentially, as she put it, she would agree to live in a golden cage, with the door firmly open, but only because she had a special regard for her clumsy lover.

The deal was sealed over dinner at Calcutta's most exclusive restaurant and a night at the Park Hotel. A few weeks after that, Tinku was engaged to be married.

He dreaded Saira's reaction, but she took it extremely well, he thought. She reminded him that nothing need change. He loved her, after all, and he owed no loyalty to the stranger who would be entering his home in a few days. Saira even came to the wedding, managing to pry him away from the ceremony for a quick 'chat', as she called it.

"You're mine. You remember that, Tarun. That woman you're marrying is nothing to you, do you understand?"

Tinku understood. He kissed her hard, knelt down and pushed his head under her sari just to show her he understood.

That night in the room with his bride, Tinku's head spun with the alcohol his friends had smuggled into his drinks. He remembered looking at the woman on the bed, as cold and as still as a marble sculpture, painted with vermillion and sandalwood, gilded with silk and gold. She looked too tricky to unwrap.

She would not look at him. He remembered that too, but he'd fuck her, nonetheless. And he did. He didn't bother after that. There was no point.

7

Tinku – 1981. Spring, Calcutta, India

On this day it was early evening before Tinku arrived at his father's house. He was emotionally and physically drained. Saira had that effect on him. He rang the bell and waited impatiently. He knew that it would be a while before anyone could walk the whole length of the rambling Calcutta property, longer if they had to descend the stairs, but eventually he began to worry that there was no one at home. He rang the bell again. This time it was opened almost instantly, by a woman he hardly recognised. He stared at the woman with skin so white it was almost translucent, and he marvelled at the realisation that this was the woman he had married. He wondered why he had not seen the woman with doe-eyes and ebony hair before, but then he supposed he was either drunk or she was asleep. Either way, he felt a pang of remorse.

Akanksha's legs almost buckled beneath her. Her husband looked different somehow today, more like the photo she had

41

seen of him before they were married. He looked like he had not shaved for a couple of days and that his nails needed trimming, but essentially the dull hardness she had experienced on previous occasions was missing now.

"Ma and Baba have gone for their evening walk," she said. "They'll be back soon."

Tinku ran a hand through his hair and asked to come inside.

"It's your house." Akanksha said quietly, and went to fetch a glass of water.

Tinku walked into the reception room, leaving his suitcase of clothes in the hall. He noticed the new rug and the vases which he could not remember seeing before and felt a tinge of guilt. How were they paying for this? Perhaps Baba's pension was enough, after all.

In the kitchen, Akanksha searched through her contacts and dialled while her heart pounded.

"Rahul, here, tell me, Mrinu."

"I can't come today."

"What do you mean? I was expecting you. What's the emergency?"

"You know that I would not cancel if it was not important. I'll tell you when I see you."

"But when will I see you?"

"I don't know."

Akanksha put the phone down and filled a steel tumbler with mineral water. She cursed herself and took out a glass from the crockery cabinet. She hoped he would appreciate some special treatment.

She placed the glass on a tray and walked out to the reception room, where she found Tinku leafing through a photo album his mother had stored on one of the shelves. He put it down as soon as Akanksha entered. He was staring more pointedly this time, making Akanksha blush. She was accustomed to being appraised by men but at those times she was expecting it and even inviting it. Tinku's stare made her feel uncomfortable.

He cleared his throat and moved towards Akanksha as she retreated towards the door.

"Come, sit down. We haven't really talked." He sat down on the sofa.

Akanksha sat down in a chair next to him.

"So, how are you finding it here?" Tinku asked. He shifted his weight, making himself more comfortable.

"It's nice. I like it here."

"Do you have any complaints?"

"No. Ma and Baba are very kind. They hardly let me do any work."

They were interrupted by the doorbell ringing again. Akanksha sprang up from her seat to answer it. It was the maid. Akanksha gave instructions to make some tea and moori, puffed rice with fried onions and green chilli, for Tinku Da, as he was known to the servants, and then rejoined her husband.

He was looking at the phone.

"Do you know any English?" he suddenly asked, looking up.

"A little. Not much. Not enough to hold a conversation."

"My English is also not brilliant, but I must speak it in the office."

Akanksha sat with her hands folded on her lap.

Their previous meeting, which was typical of their marriage, consisted of Tinku pushing past her to grab some ironed shirts from the armoire in their room. She set about refolding the clothes her husband had thrown on the bed in an attempt to find the stash of bills that were usually hidden on the top shelf. Every visit home Tinku would place some bills there. He never said why or what she should do with them. She never touched them, believing them to be his. That day, he seemed to need the cash desperately, desperately enough to spare a few words for Akanksha. He accused her of stealing the money, of spending it on something frivolous. Akanksha listened and continued folding. Suddenly Tinku stopped ranting. He became still on the chair he was balanced on. He came down slowly and walked to the bed. He checked under the mattress and produced a wad of notes. Without a word, he placed them in his wallet, took his suitcase and walked out of the door and out of the house.

Today he looked at her as he spoke. He asked her questions as if he were meeting her for the first time. She longed for her in-laws to come home so the attention would be taken away from her.

A long ten minutes later the maid arrived with the tea, just as the doorbell rang once more. This time, Akanksha opened the door and sighed with relief.

Her mother-in-law saw the suitcase in the hallway and rushed into the room where her son was sipping his tea. There was a long embrace and then Tinku touched the feet of both his parents. The joy in his father's eyes at seeing his son made Akanksha a little jealous. She could not remember anyone looking at her this way.

Quietly, she withdrew, making her way into the kitchen again. The maid was washing the dishes from earlier in the day. There was a cup of tea waiting for her and Akanksha gulped it down gratefully. The maid smiled fondly at her. She made another two cups for Akanksha's mother-in-law and father-in-law and then drank her own tea in a cup that had been assigned to her.

Eventually Akanksha's mother-in-law made her way into the kitchen, barking orders. Akanksha was sent upstairs to get the bedroom ready, with strict instructions to unpack her husband's things carefully.

She willingly escaped, glad of the solitude. The suitcase had already been brought up and Akanksha knelt down to undo the zip.

As she walked back down the stairs with the peeling paint work, the crumbling plaster on the walls reminded her of all that still needed repairing, patching up in the house that had become her home. Carpenters had already been called for the kitchen cabinets, and work would begin at the beginning of next month. Now she could add plasterwork and painting to the list. She could hear Tinku's voice on the phone in the hallway, and the voices coming from the television as her mother-in-law settled down into her routine.

"Look, you can't call me here. You know my parents could have picked up."

Pause.

"I'll call you after midnight."

Pause.

"Why can't you understand?"

Pause.

"I love only you. I haven't even seen her. How many times do I have to tell you?"

Pause.

"I have to go. Goodbye. I love you."

There was a knot in Akanksha's stomach. Why did she feel a sense of betrayal?

She continued downstairs, surprising Tinku. He quickly placed the phone back into its cradle and looked at her. She walked into the kitchen and picked up some of the change she had left there from before and calmly went back up the stairs. Tinku was waiting for her, sitting on the bed.

"How much did you hear?" There was none of the gentle curiosity that she had seen earlier. This tone was harsh.

"I heard enough."

"My parents cannot find out. Do you understand?"

"Yes. Am I to leave? Would you like a divorce?"

The thought that perhaps he could release Akanksha, that she could leave, if she wished or he wished had not crossed his mind.

"Is that what you would like?" he asked.

"I don't know."

She could begin a whole new life somewhere, somewhere she was not known and had no obligations. There would be no one to please, no ties. But then she thought about her mother-in-law. She would never agree. The arrangement was working too well.

Tinku was thinking how happy Saira would be.

He thought about marrying Saira and beginning a real married life. The secrecy, the constant leaving and lying were wearing on him. He was not enjoying it anymore.

The idea of a divorce, a fresh start was appealing to him more and more. He would need to seek some advice, he decided.

8

1981. Spring, Calcutta, India

She sat as if she held a stringed instrument; her left leg folded under her right, which was bent upwards, her knee pointing to the ceiling. Her hair flowed in brown waves, down her straight back and painted on her forehead was an orb of vermillion, a slightly smudged yet perfect circle. Today she was Mrinamayi.

Mrinamayi sat watching, perfectly still, perfectly straight. Her figure cast a silhouette in the window in the pose of Meerabai, Lord Krishna's devotee in love with the unattainable. Her sari was a simple white cotton, edged with gold, falling just short of covering her waist. Her eyes were all that moved, darting from one person to the next. They did not see her.

She wondered what they said. They spoke English and then some Hindi and then English again. She recognised the languages, but not the words, although she was learning.

Most of the people in the room were lying on the floor, resting on their elbows, facing each other. Her 'friend', as he referred to himself, was on the sofa. He looked like a prince holding court. Mrinamayi felt a touch of pride. It was misplaced, she knew, but for now she was his and he was hers.

On her ankles she wore gold chains and solitaires shone in her earlobes. From toe to head, Mrinamayi looked like a princess.

The whirring fan blew a stray lock of hair across her mouth. Her lips were painted with a shade of deep rose, as if stained with forest berries. She moved the strand of hair away, making the gold bangles on her wrist to jingle. It brought her to his attention.

"Go and wait in the bedroom, Mrinu, I'll be with you shortly."

Mrinamayi rose gracefully and walked towards the bedroom. She paused at the door, glancing back. He was kissing one of the women, a long passionate kiss. A pang of jealousy shot through Mrinamayi, flew up and out, and landed like a bird just out of reach, mocking her. She shooed it away just as their lips unlocked, and she entered the bedroom alone. She fingered the mussed silk bedclothes, and then walked to the balcony door to see the sun rising. From the next room she could hear a series of 'goodbyes' and 'see you laters' and longed for it to end. All she wanted was to lie down and sleep; to not be touched. But she dared not slip into the covers without his permission.

The door opened, and he walked in. He undid the buttons on his shirt, walked over to her. She knew not to react, he preferred to make the first move. He pulled her towards him and bit her lip. She gasped in pain. Slowly, he proceeded to unwrap her like a gift and fling her on the bed.

Tinku sat with Saira on the veranda. It overlooked the cigarette stall where the men bought their cigarettes, sometimes one at a time and sometimes by the packet. Sometimes Tinku would go down and buy a packet of Goldflake Lights, which he would share with Saira in the night. He loved to watch her smoke and melt into the swirls of vapour before emerging like a genie as the cloud dissipated. He loved the way she held the tip to her mouth, like Marilyn Monroe, her eyelids languid and heavy. At moments like this she was softer than the snarling, demanding creature he knew by day.

She allowed him to rest his head on her lap and watch the dark sky above them. Sometimes they could see the moon, but they rarely saw the stars.

"But who needs stars?" Saira would say when Tinku complained, "We make our own luck."

Tinku wanted this moment to last forever but he knew her moods and how they could change suddenly.

"I have to go tomorrow. I'll be going back home for a week."

Saira stopped stroking his hair and sat up straight, forcing Tinku to sit up too.

"This is your home."

"No, I mean my father's home, darling." Tinku took Saira's hand and brought it to his lips, hoping to appease her. She did not respond.

"I will try and come back sooner but you know how it is, na?"

"I know only what I see. They still control you. You don't need to see them at all, but every month it's the same!" Saira's voice was sharp, her fists were clenched.

"Look, Saira, be reasonable—"

"Why wait until the morning? Go now. Just take your things and go! I will have nothing more to do with you!"

Tinku sighed. Early on in their relationship, this would terrify him. He would believe that it had all ended. He would sleep on the sofa in the apartment living room and go out the next day to buy an expensive item of jewellery. Saira would smile at last and they would spend the rest of the daylight hours in bed; finally he would have permission to leave.

However, his friends had pointed out that a woman like Saira would not let a cash-cow like Tinku go so easily. She would lose everything and would have to begin again somewhere else if Tarun Majumdar were to leave her life, and which fool would want to start all over again? Tinku nodded. His Saira was certainly no fool.

So the next time Saira informed Tinku that she would no longer have him in her life, Tinku quietly packed his bags, walked out of the front door, and pressed the button to call the lift. Saira, confused, asked Tinku what he thought he was doing.

With a trembling lip, Tinku replied: "I am leaving you, my love, just as you have desired it."

Saira had thought of a response before the lift reached the ground floor. She had a message waiting for him at the front desk stating that she would leave the key with Security, and she would take only her clothes and jewellery. She asked him not to worry, that she would be out by the end of the week and she and her unborn child would survive somehow.

Tinku heard the message but only absorbed it as he walked to the main road to hail a cab. Immediately, he turned and ran back to Rajanigandha Apartments. He ran up the stairs to the sixth floor and pounded on the door. All at once, out of breath and delirious with joy, Tinku embraced Saira and then fell at her feet, hugging her legs like a toddler clinging to his mother.

"Why did you not tell me sooner? You are my life. Please don't leave me!"

9

Today she was Sheila. Her ponytail was high and her lipstick, a bright red. Her false nails were talons and she wore red stilettos, a little wobbly. This was what he wanted her to look like when they were out together.

Today Subhash was to meet her at the hotel. The pale morning sun cast a pleasant warmth on Sheila's bare arms as she basked outside the Taj. Her oversized sunglasses and her undersized skirt, with the backdrop of the city's cloudless blue sky, made her feel like a starlet. She had grown used to wearing skirts and shorts, although, not too long ago it would have been unthinkable. The security guards kept their distance. They knew who she was, what she was, and it was not their place to judge – but she would not be allowed inside without an actual guest.

She saw Subhash's car as it entered the gates and made sure she turned away, giving the impression that she had not seen him after all. She had learned to play games. It made it easier to pretend the skin she inhabited, the lips which were touched, were not her own.

She thought now and then about her mother and her words to her before she gave her away to her husband's family. To live with honour, to always keep her self-respect, and to please her husband. She was proud that her daughter would be able to hold her head up in society, that she would be called someone's wife, and that her daughter's children would know their father. It was a blessing too great to be squandered, her mother told her. This marriage truly was a miracle, in her mother's eyes. What family would accept a girl with no father?

Subhash stepped out of his car, not waiting for his driver to open the door for him. His round body was like a barrel, Sheila thought. His thick black handlebar moustache covered his upper lip and disguised his buck teeth. His spectacles too were thick and black rimmed, reminding one of the intellectual heroes of Bengali cinema. He was a combination of softness and hair and he seemed to be in constant apology.

At first Sheila was repulsed by the man, but she had grown to like him. Subhash could not make love to his wife. Erectile dysfunction, they called it. He thought being with someone other than his wife would help him but it did not. He had been advised to take herbal remedies, which also did not help him. Sheila was thankful. It meant that this was a holiday of sorts.

Subhash enjoyed talking. He talked and talked over expensive meals and wines, which Sheila barely touched. He told her stories about his workers and their families and the lies they told him when they wanted a holiday or the audacious rates they would quote when they overcharged him for the building materials for his projects. He told her about his wife who wanted children so badly she cried herself to sleep every night and he told her about the guilt of not being able to give her those children.

Today, as Sheila looked out of a window in another expensive restaurant, she felt the urge to to reach out to someone who only wanted a friend. He gave the impression that he trusted her.

"Have you been to see a proper doctor? Someone who specialises in these things?"

Subhash raised his eyebrows and coughed into his coffee.

"My wife has asked me to several times, Sheila. But to be honest with you, I am terrified of what they may say. I have even tried special herbal treatments and medicines and even this does not help."

"Perhaps it is not real medicine. There are many cheats here, in this country of ours," replied Sheila quietly, as she picked at watermelon on her plate.

"Perhaps you are right. But the shame of it! Is it not shameful to be a man and not be a man?"

"You men have strange ideas of what is shameful and what is not. To have an illness is not shameful, Subhash. As someone who has seen many men, I know you most certainly are a man."

"Do you think I should go?" Desperation crept into his voice.

"Yes, I think you should go."

"Then I will. I'll go tomorrow." He bit hard into his croissant.

He took out a jewellery box and asked Sheila to open it. She did so, feigning surprise and gratitude. She placed the gold bracelet on her wrist and asked Subhash to fasten the clasp.

"You have been such a comfort to me, Sheila. I enjoy buying you things."

"And I cannot lie, Subhash. I enjoy your company and I enjoy your gifts." Sheila flashed her client a rare smile. That was all he wanted from her for now and it was easy to give.

Subhash regarded Sheila. There was a physical attraction at the beginning, but now there was a desire to take care of her and protect her. Although she smiled and said the right things, she rarely looked happy. It made him feel guilty. He knew if his wife found out she would be devastated but he hadn't thought of how Sheila must feel, to be forced to enter into this arrangement with a fat, impotent Bengali Babu. She was beautiful, how ashamed must she be to be seen with him?

He took her hand and looked into her eyes.

"If all goes well tomorrow at the doctor's, I want to do something for you. Something that will change your life. Will you let me?"

"Yes." she said.

There really was a life growing inside Saira. She had let it happen. She had stopped taking the pill a few months ago and although her periods were heavier and more painful for a time, she delighted in the feeling of freedom. Once they stopped completely, Saira was elated, wishing her mother was there to share the news.

It was early morning, the sun still had not risen fully in the sky. No one was up yet, not even the birds who sang distractingly every morning. Saira woke up with a slight feeling of nausea. There was a packet of digestive biscuits on her bedside table and Saira took one to appease the sudden hunger, washing it down with a glass of water. Tinku lay beside her. He had put on weight in the time she had known him, making him look less like a bumbling teenager and more like a man.

She would not tell him yet. She would wait until after dinner. She was not sure when she had become so dependent on the man in her bed, it had happened gradually, without her realising. She despised his wife, and knew that Tinku was indifferent to her, wanting only Saira. Even after all this time, they needed to be careful of how they were in front of others. His friends knew, and even some of his relatives, but not his parents. They might decide to disown their only son and then Saira would have been working towards an empty dream. But she did not want to be hidden and pointed at or judged anymore.

She watched Tinku sleep. He had oil in his hair, staining the pillow covers a darker shade than they were meant to be.

He had been complaining of a headache so Saira massaged oil in expertly, her fingers following the shape of his skull. She told him how her mother would do the same for her when she was studying. Some days her father would bring home jasmine flowers to place in her and her mother's hair, filling their tiny house with a heady scent that would linger all day. When her mother died, Saira stopped wearing flowers in her hair. For a while she continued to study. She was going to do something with her life she had told her mother and her mother believed her; it was difficult to concentrate now she was gone, and easier to let the boys take her behind the chemistry lab to make love to her. She did not need to concentrate for that and somehow it made the emptiness feel a little less overwhelming.

Her results were not good. They were worse than mediocre and the only colleges she could get into were not what she had hoped for at all. Saira went to Calcutta. When she left, her father saw her off at the train station with a tiffin carrier of lemon rice and curd. He had made it himself, waking early, boiling the rice, stirring in the sautéed spices, peanuts and lemon. It was his way of saying he loved her, still. But there was no other sign. She touched his feet and boarded the train. She never saw him again. Any desire she had to be close to her father was fulfilled by a telephone call.

Some time ago, Saira had fallen in love. He was an older man. He would let his fingers linger over her skin, he would kiss her as if her were tasting her, and she mistook it all for love. She gave her heart to him but snatched it back, bruised and damaged, when she found out that he had a wife he would not leave.

The time was right for the child. She looked forward to watching herself expand. She would be thin again, afterwards and she would be a good mother. She would make sure her daughter or son did well. They would call her Amma, and they would finish a meal with plain curd and rice, without sugar, as was proper, not like Tinku who would mix a whole tablespoon of sugar, corrupting the taste and value of the curd. If it was a girl, she would ask Tinku to buy flowers for their hair.

10

Anjana was tall and brash. She liked to wear saris the colour of the sea in Mumbai, with gold embroidery and sparkly borders. Her eyes were rimmed with kohl and her bindi caught the sunlight every time she cocked her head. She had the look of someone who mocked everything, as if she was always stifling a smile.

"Rupaiyya dao na, Saab? Apke pas bohut kuch hai. Humare ko bhi de do!" she would ask the rich men in their chauffer driven cars of foreign make. *Give me some money, na, Sir. You have so much, why not share a little with me?*

Sometimes they would and sometimes they would not. But when they would, the men received a wink and smile as she delicately placed the note under the strap of her bra before moving swiftly to the next vehicle.

By midday Anjana was weary of standing there, and the traffic had not slowed long enough for her to make as much as she normally did. She scratched the stubble on her face and adjusted her sari blouse. The padding that had been sewn in was slipping out; she would have to speak to the tailor again. The lecherous man could not help brushing up against her crotch, feeling for her testicles, and Anjana could do nothing except slap the man who took it as a sign of playful defiance. Unfortunately, there was no one else close by who would do the work so she tolerated it.

Anjana wondered if she should stop over at Aunty's house for some gossip and tea. There was a chance that Mrinu might be there, as it was a Friday.

She walked to the side of the road, took out her cash, and counted it, her long fingers separating the notes deftly. They stopped when they came across a piece of white paper with a number and a name on. She sounded out the Bengali letters, then sighed and tore up the piece of paper, letting the pieces fall. She started counting again. She could always come back, she thought. She would have to come back.

Alok, the paan waala, sat under his giant umbrella. Anjana walked over and ordered a paan, took out a ten rupee note and waited as Alok did his magic. She watched him as she leaned up against the side of a hut and admired the way his strong, dark forearms glistened. His forehead was beaded with minuscule droplets of sweat, which Anjana ached to wipe away with the end of her sari. The green betel leaf shone and sparkled like a jewel as Alok placed it, freshly rinsed, on his table. He applied the white chalky lime and chopped the supari into tiny red shreds of flavour. He added some zarda and folded the paan into a neat triangular gem. Anjana placed the triangle in her mouth and gave Alok the cash. As she waited for the four-rupee change she asked him, with the paan firmly stuffed in her right cheek, whether Alok wanted to watch a movie with her.

He did not look up. Instead he grunted something and shooed Anjana away with his hand.

"Your loss," she sighed, and walked away.

The path was orangey-red and dry beneath her sandaled feet. Sand found its way in between her toes and under her soles, making it uncomfortable. However, this discomfort she could handle. She was accustomed to walking and did not feel like shelling out another couple of notes for a rickshaw ride, although the sun was high. It was about a twenty-minute walk and she was sure she would meet someone else along the way to keep her company; she usually did. On second thoughts, perhaps she would like to walk alone today. She chewed thoughtfully as she strolled on the side of the road, narrowly escaping the autos, hand-drawn carts, cycle-rickshaws and yellow cabs. She thought she resembled a cow as her lower jaw moved up and down, side to side, so she tried to chew in a more elegant manner, like she imagined her friend Mrinu would chew. She hadn't seen Mrinu in a long time; she enjoyed their meetings. They spoke almost in whispers so as not to wake Aunty, in whose house they met. Friday was bookkeeping day. Mrinu would pay her fees to Aunty and Anjana would pay hers. They would brief Aunty about their clients and Aunty would tell them what was to come. Aunty then would take her rice, roll out a mat, and fall asleep on the floor as a maid pressed her legs and massaged her feet.

The last two Fridays, Mrinu had come and gone early. Aunty did not care to ask why, meaning Anjana never found out, so as Anjana opened the crooked iron gate of Aunty's house, she squealed with delight when she saw Mrinu's skin shining in the dark front room of the house with no doors.

Anjana hugged her friend and was relieved to feel Mrinu reciprocate. It had only been three weeks, but it felt like so much longer. She looked at her and noticed that the roundness, the softness, was slowly disappearing. Her eyes look tired.

"What happened to you, friend?"

"Nothing much. I'll tell you later. Aunty is calling us. Come."

The three women sat cross-legged on the dry, clean, clay floor. Their knees were touching and the faint aroma of Anjana's chewing tobacco from her paan and the fragrance of the flowers in Aunty's hair filled the room. A black and white cat wandered in and mewed curiously at them. Aunty picked up her fan and shooed it away.

"You both are my gems. You both are my Lakshmis in my old age. Look at me, girls, who would want me? But look at the both of you." She stroked Mrinu's face and let her fingers linger longer than was comfortable. "You would not dare to make an old woman unhappy, now would you?"

Anjana caught the menace in the glance and tone. What stupidity had Mrinu done now?

"Your friend, Subhash has offered to buy you out, my dear. He's offered to take you away and release you, like a white dove, into the blue sky."

Mrinu looked up, startled at the revelation. Slowly, the realisation spread across her face and Anjana could see her piecing together bits of a conversation that she must have had.

"I'm sorry, Aunty, I did not know. I did not ask for this. This is the only life I have. Please don't do anything to change this. This... this works for everyone."

Aunty studied Mrinamayi's face. "I will give you one more chance so listen to me carefully. This stupid sadness you carry around with you, it must stop. People can see it. People will either be turned off by you or they will feel sorry for you and try to do what Subhash Babu has tried to do for you. You are not doing yourself any favours, my dear. You won't last long. Your beauty is already fading."

Aunty turned to Anjana this time, "You explain. You've been doing this for a long time. She's only had a year or so."

Anjana looked pleadingly at her friend and saw that Aunty was right. There was a fragile hollowness about her now that reminded Anjana of the glass vials of perfume they sold on the corner of Ezra Street. Anjana agreed with Aunty, for once: this could not go on.

⁕

Tinku sat with his feet up on the coffee table in front of the television. The flashing images from the screen lit up his face and body. He looked up and blinked, removed his spectacles and rubbed his eyes with the heel of his hand.

"I wasn't listening, what did you say, my love?"

"I'm pregnant. About twelve weeks."

Tinku turned off the television and knelt at Saira's feet.

"Are you sure?"

"I've been to the doctor. He has confirmed it."

"I'll tell my family I want a divorce. I don't need them. I'll tell them about you."

"You would do that?"

"You know I would."

"Then do it."

That night, they made love to each other.

Tinku waited until his parents were out and then he rang the bell. He waited patiently for Akanksha to open the door.

Somewhere, a conch shell was being blown just as the door was opened, momentarily making Tinku think that something epic was happening. It made his resolve stronger. Initially, after speaking to his mother, he had felt defeated. She had not agreed to Tinku getting a divorce. In fact she had ignored Tinku's wishes altogether and had made it clear that he would need to move back home and start contributing financially. Tinku mentally prepared himself for telling Saira that things would just have to continue as they were. But Saira had made it plain, she wanted more now. She was tired of being a ghost.

He would deal directly with Akanksha. He would accept

full responsibility and just need her to sign agreeing to the terms.

Akanksha led Tinku into the reception room where he sat at the edge of the sofa. He did not look comfortable and this time he did not look at her the way he had the last time. Whatever interest he had in her before was gone now. He tapped his foot nervously against the tiled floor and his hand shook as Akanksha handed him a glass of water.

"I have something to tell you."

"Then tell me."

"I am living with another woman."

"I know that already."

"Of course you do. Sorry. But you also need to know that I will be giving you a divorce. You will just have to sign a piece of paper and then you will be free of me. I am sure Ma and Baba will keep you on here, but you will no longer be obligated to me."

"Why now?"

Akanksha's fingers played with the end of her sari, wringing the fabric until it was creased and then smoothing it out, only to repeat the process.

"She is having my child. We want it to have a legitimate home. We don't want him or her to grow up in shame."

"I can see that. Very well. If you have the papers, I will sign them now."

Only Akanksha's hands betrayed any signs of distress. Tinku shook his head.

"I will come back tomorrow at this time. What would you

like financially? I cannot give you much. I'll have a family to support."

"What about this family?"

"Just tell me what you want, and you can have it."

"I want nothing from you. I am not planning on staying after the divorce. Ask your parents what they would like. Ask them after I am gone. I have been working to support them. I do not plan to continue with the line of work your mother has chosen for me."

Tinku was relieved. He did not even think to ask about Akanksha's line of work. To him, it no longer mattered what she did. He would be free of her.

"Do you know what's ironic?"

"Hm?" Tinku was distracted, his eyes on the door.

"Nothing. It doesn't matter."

He got up to leave. There was no kiss goodbye, no embrace, no handshake. He just looked back once as she waved slightly at the door.

Saira was waiting in the cab when Tinku appeared. He did not look as happy as she would have liked, but for now she would let him be. She only asked if it was done and he told her that it was. He would be back tomorrow with the papers to sign. She wanted nothing from him.

Saira, relieved, leant back against the lumpy leather seats. She held her stomach tightly as the cab manoeuvred its way through roads cratered with potholes. Tinku was still, on the far side. He lit up a cigarette and blew smoke out of the window. That was it then. He probably would never see his family home again: the mint green walls and the rosewood furniture; the mother, the father, the wife; the teas and the food; the politics and the tears. He looked at Saira. Her eyes were closed, her arms wrapped around her middle, protecting the child within. She looked as if she were asleep but suddenly she looked at him. She gave him her hand and he held it, squeezed it tightly until they were both sure of what that meant.

11

1981: Summer, Calcutta, India

"Mrinu, why didn't you come last week? You know you made me very angry!"

"If I tell you, Rahul, what will it accomplish? Let it be, na? What we have is good."

"You're a wily one! What do you think? I know you're not as pure as snow. I know you must have other clients, but you have never stood me up for someone else, we have our days and they have theirs, so, what was it?"

"Kiss me."

"Gladly. Now tell me."

"Can I ask you something?"

"Only if I get an answer first."

"But my answer is dependent on your answer."

"You win! What do you want to know?"

"Can you love me? can you make me yours, in the eyes of the world?"

"You know I can't. What are you? Stupid?"

The mood was ruined. The lights were turned back on and the candles extinguished, all in a heartbeat. Mrinu sighed. She did not mean for this to happen. She shifted her weight off the bed, walked to the mirror, rewrapped herself in the crumpled cotton sari and straightened the bindi on her forehead. She brushed her hair and picked up her bag.

"I need to go. Our time is up. I'll see you next week."

Rahul stood behind her. He looked at their reflection in the mirror. Picture perfect. He would have liked to have someone like Mrinu is his life, but everyone knew who she was here. He would have to begin again somewhere new if it were to work. His friends already teased him about his softness with her, the way he trusted her and treated her too well. He was able to disregard them because they were his friends, but colleagues, bosses, parents, uncles... they could not so easily be ignored. His mother had caught wind of the rumours that her son was paying for the services of a 'working girl' and she took it as a sign to start looking for a bride for him. Her eldest was already married and had produced beautiful grandchildren, worthy of the family they were born into. Rahul had only given them scandal.

"Look, don't be angry. You are very special to me, but it won't work. My life is already a disappointment in my mother's eyes, imagine what would happen if I married you? They would disown me, my bosses would demote me, and my friends would leave me."

Mrinu nodded. "Our twenty-four hours were up two

hours ago. Any longer and I will have to start charging you overtime," Mrinu spoke as sweetly as her emotions would allow, tempering the hurt in her voice. She picked up her handbag and walked out, closing the door behind her.

Her sandals flapped noisily in the evening on the pavement as she walked to the bus stop. She realised too late she had made a big mistake. It was entirely possible that Rahul would now ask for someone else. She had been deluded into thinking that he could offer her a way out, that he thought more of her. She wondered if Anjana could give her some advice. There was no one else on her side and she had told Anjana everything the last time they met, and Anjana had encouraged her to find a way out. Surely there was something else she could do, other than sell her body.

Her bus arrived and Mrinu clambered on, jogging slightly to catch up with the CTC bus that would only slow, never stop. She managed to find a seat after a polite looking businessman got up for her. He looked at his shoes, too modest to look into her eyes.

There was nothing else for it, she decided: she would have to run away. She pictured it happening in the dead of night, as the house slept. It would be easier when Tinku was away, but he was staying for longer than normal during this visit. Meanwhile she would have to start preparing, hoarding her cash, finding her PAN card and ration card, which mother-in-law held somewhere in a safe in the house. She thought about her father-in-law and wondered if she should finally tell him the truth about what was happening under his own roof. She would miss the old man, but he only loved a version of her that was as ephemeral as news he read every morning.

The bus came to a halt a few yards from her home. She jumped as the bus was still moving and steadied herself as her feet hit the ground. Somewhere dogs barked as if in a fight, a neighbour called from her balcony for her daughter to come in, and Mrs Sen was getting out of her car, hands laden with shopping bags. Familiarity had suddenly become alien and Akanksha felt like a stranger.

She reached for the doorbell and then remembered to check for her key. She had it, this time, at the bottom of the front zipped portion. She fumbled to reach it and pulled out Subhash's card. He may still agree to help her, she thought.

Inside the television was on. She walked in and saw her mother-in-law staring at a screen, jaw slack, eyes wide. Someone was crying on screen and Akanksha noticed that her mother-in-law's eyes were also damp. Akanksha cleared her throat and waited for the older woman to look up. When eventually she did, a deep sadness filled her face.

"Tinku is having an affair."

Akanksha knew to feign surprise. The hurt and betrayal she still inexplicably felt was genuine. She flopped down on the sofa, her shoes still on, her bag on her arm. She allowed tears to fall against her cheeks and into the hollow of her neck.

"But you must not be too sad. I have told him he cannot divorce you. You will always be a part of this family. I have also told him that he needs to start paying his way a little more. I have had enough of his irresponsible behaviour. Needless to say, my dear, he has packed his bags and gone to stay with that hussy! He'll be back though, with his dirty laundry and his cravings for my mustard fish curry."

More tears fell; nothing had changed; everything was as it was. A part of her had hoped that if Tinku left the other woman, they could begin a normal life. She could grow to love him, the man who showed a gentle affection, who was curious about her, who would stare at her, sometimes in awe. Perhaps she could be happy with him. Perhaps then, her mother-in-law would ask her to stay at home, as was proper for a daughter-in-law of a respected family.

Akanksha, head bowed, left the room, leaving the money on the table. Her mother-in-law resumed her viewing. Somewhere, deep inside Akanksha the flame was being stoked and her resolve was growing: she would not stay here for much longer.

"Mrinu, are you sure you want to do this? She'll send someone looking for you!"

"I know, but she won't find me. I'll leave her what I can and that should keep her happy for a while. I'm sure she'll find someone else."

"I don't see what the problem is. You get paid, it's safe, you're working with high class clients and one of them you're not even fucking. What is your problem?"

"My problem is, this is not where I saw my life heading. I saw a husband who loved me, I saw children and loving grandparents for them, I saw me holding my head up high for once, of being able to let go of the shame of not knowing my father."

"Life's not like that, Mrinu. It's not a TV series where we all look hot and always get the guys we fall in love with. There are no demons and angels who thwart us or rescue us. This is our lot and we make the best of it."

"I'm tired of just letting things happen to me, Anjana. All my life decisions have been made for me."

Anjana blew out smoke from the bidi. She held it between her finger and thumb and inhaled again, eyes scrunched up, lips pursed. She was quiet for a time, letting her thoughts escape up into the air, letting them mingle with the grey of the smoke. Lightheaded and melancholic, this is how she felt at this moment. She would be losing her only friend and she wasn't even sure her friend was making the right decision for herself.

"You can't speak Hindi, where will you go?"

"I can understand a little, enough to get by. Or perhaps I'll travel north, where there will be more Bengalis like me. I could contact my mother, ask if there are any relatives I can stay with. I would work for my food and board."

"I don't think you've thought this through."

"I'm thinking now. I'm not planning on leaving straight away. I need to find my documents first."

"Listen, if you run, you shouldn't run as yourself. I know

74

someone who can get you new documents, a new name."

Mrinu hugged her friend. Both had tears in their eyes.

"Then you will help me?"

"If this is what you have decided on, Mrinu. But think carefully, who will you be? What will you do?"

"I can be anyone I choose, and I can do anything I want."

12

Mrinamayi lay on the bed. This would be the last time she would be doing this, she thought. She made a special effort to take in her surroundings and commit them to memory: the scent of the bedclothes, the light pouring into every corner. She would not miss Rahul so much; she would miss the fresh smell of the bathroom after he bathed and she would miss sometimes watching him cook, when he was in the mood. He would make pancakes, with a squeeze of lime and a pinch of sugar, resembling the dosas from the south, so that she expected something savoury. She did not like them at first, but later came to crave them. She had them with a cup of coffee, milky and sweet. Rahul preferred it black without sugar. She tasted it once, on his insistence and resisted the urge to spit it back out.

"Drink it all," he commanded. She took it like a medicine. Rahul laughed at her. He called her uncouth, unsophisticated, and made love to her roughly that time, making sure she called out in pain. "You're nothing but a peasant," he jeered with his teeth bared and his weight on top of her.

There would be no more of his jibes, thought Mrinu, in a quiet voice to herself. She debated whether to take anything. There were bits of jewellery on the dressing table: a pair of earrings, a chain, a hair tie; a bottle of perfume, her hairbrush, a pack of red bindis. He had bought all of these things for her, giving the illusion she shared the property with Rahul, but time and again she was reminded that it was not the case. She would take nothing, she decided.

She waited patiently for Rahul to finish in the bathroom and then she would take a shower. She would wash her hair today, with the expensive shampoo he bought for her, wash off the sindoor in the parting of her hair and leave strands carelessly strewn across the floor of the shower. After that she would apply the face cream bought by Rahul and the lipstick and the powder. She liked the idea of him not knowing, for once, her being in control. Her mother once told her to enjoy the simple things and this surely was the simplest of all, to be in control.

Akanksha was not sure what it was that she was doing. Her plan to escape was sketchy, at best. There was no detail, no allowances for eventualities beyond her control. It was a basic 'catch the first train out of here' kind of plan but she was aware that she would need help.

Thanks to a friend of Tinku's the divorce had happened, rushed through the civil courts. One kind of freedom, at least, had been granted her. There was now nothing legally binding her to the man whom she did not love. His parents still did not know. Her mother-in-law was unpredictable and Akanksha didn't feel that she would gain anything from telling the old woman. Akanksha was sure she blamed her for not being able to please her son. One day Akanksha had overheard her mother-in-law speaking to one of her closest friends on the phone, asking for her opinion. Did she think her son did not like women? Her friend must have reassured her that Tinku did like women, very much, since her reaction made Tinku's mother cackle with laughter and admit that her friend was right.

Akanksha could not find her documents, though she had scoured the house.

Now Akanksha knocked on the door to her ex-husband's apartment. She waited. The door was opened by a woman whose belly was ripe and round.

"Come in." The voice was sweet, a slight accent was there, enough to make it interesting though, not comic.

From the back, the woman looked thin. There seemed to be no indication of her hips or her waist. It was only from the side or the front that her contours showed she was expecting a child. Akanksha felt again the envy she had felt when Tinku revealed that he was to be a father. She held on to it, thinking somehow that it gave her comfort.

"Would you like some tea?"

"No. I came to speak my—"

To call him her ex-husband seemed wrong, somehow; he had barely ever been a husband.

"I've come to speak with Tarun."

"He's out. He won't be back until late. I do not want him speaking to you. Tell me what you want, and I may be able to help you."

"I don't know what I want."

"You know you have no right to be here, don't you? There is nothing that we are obliged to give you. You signed a document saying you wanted nothing from him."

"I know. But I have no one else. I just need some advice."

Saira looked at the woman before her. She hated the helplessness she seemed to exude. With everything that she had been given, she was still stupid, dependent and powerless.

The baby kicked inside her. The kicks were getting stronger now. Sometimes, if she watched she would see an elbow or knee on her abdomen. One day, she was sure she saw the impression of a foot, five tiny toes, a heel. She was getting impatient, wanting to hold the little one, the being that would love her unconditionally; there were days when Saira cried because she just wanted her mother to be there, to see her becoming a mother herself.

Akanksha saw the change in Saira's expression, the softening, the distraction. She guessed what was happening when Saira's hand involuntarily moved to her stomach. Envy again.

"I want to run away from the city. I want a new life where I am no-one's wife or daughter-in-law. I have no papers, I think Tarun's mother may have destroyed them."

"Well you'll need those first."

"Yes, but where should I go? My Hindi is very weak, and I do not speak English."

"How should I know?" Saira was growing impatient. "Do you have any skills? You'll have to work."

"My mother taught me how to cook. I can clean, I can do anything that does not require too much education."

Saira laughed. Why bother running away, she wondered, when she could do all of that, here, in Calcutta? Suddenly she felt pity for Akanksha. There really was nothing she could offer her.

"Look after yourself and yourself only. Trust no one. And men, well, they are your key to happiness or sadness, it's up to you which door you want to open. Screw them for all they've got, my dear, and then move on. You make your own destiny, there is no need to rely on them for anything." As she said this, it felt like a betrayal against Tinku. "What I'm trying to say is, trust in yourself. Only you can give you what you want, what you need."

Saira got up and walked to the bedroom. She brought out a notepad and a pen and wrote down an address.

"These people are very good. I have known them from childhood. I went to school with their daughter. It was she who inspired me to come to Calcutta. We were supposed to come together but she eloped to be married before she could sit her exams. They are a Bengali family. They will help you. Just tell them that Saira Murthy is a friend of yours. No need to go into any details." She laughed at her own joke.

"Hyderabad is not a bad city. Your Hindi will have to improve, but in the meantime these people will be able to help you settle in."

Akanksha was not sure what to say. 'Thank you' seemed inadequate. A plan, a destination, a contact. She had given her hope.

"You may as well stay and have some tea," said Saira.

Mrinu waited at the bus stop where she had been asked to wait. Anjana was running late, which was not unusual. She watched the tiny ants scurry around her sandals and thought how easy it would be to squash them underfoot. The sun was going down earlier now, leaving the air cold, especially after the rain. The mosquitoes were biting and left red marks on her skin. Her mother used to call them kisses; the bites looked more severe than they were, and her mother said it was because her blood was sweeter and her skin fairer than anyone else's. That was long before Mrinu became Mrinu, before she knew there could be such a life.

She decided to wait for another five minutes. She was just getting ready to leave when she saw the frame of her friend jogging towards her. Her sari was hitched up and she moved her head from side to side in an exaggerated manner. A rush of affection coursed through Mrinu.

"Where have you been?" she chided, "I was about to leave!"

They embraced, wiping away the tears in each other's eyes.

"Don't ask!" came Anjana's reply, "I've run all the way here from the tailor. I kicked him in the nuts this time. He won't be hassling me again. I told myself that if Mrinu is not going to take any more shit from anyone, neither am I!"

They laughed loudly, not caring what passers-by might be thinking. It would be their final goodbye to each other and the time for discretion had passed.

Anjana handed Mrinu the documents that she had promised and told her to keep them safely in her bag. Mrinu did as she was told. She refused to look at them, saying that she trusted Anjana completely.

They took the next bus to Kalighat. They would pay their respects to the Goddess before Mrinu left. They alighted at the intersection just before the main Kalighat footpath, then walked past the stalls selling idols and flowers and pots of vermillion and colours, their arms linked. Although people stared, no one bothered them. The last time Mrinu came here, she was Akanksha, the daughter-in-law, and she was suspected of having the means to give to the beggars who crawled and hobbled for some loose change. Today, she was the same as the beggars as she walked with her friend, the outcast. They were all outcasts, on this night. The goddess would appreciate that, she thought.

Mrinu stopped at a stall selling bangles traditionally worn by Bengali brides. She picked up a white one, made from conch shells, examined it and put it back. Next she picked up a red one, the colour of blood and sindoor.

"What does it mean?" she asked Anjana as she turned away from the stall. "Marriage, what does it mean? I never saw a happy one."

"In our line of work, for the kind of people we are, my love, there is no place for a happy marriage. Perhaps you will find it where you are going."

"I don't think I want to look. I would like to explore what it is like to be me, first."

"A grand idea, Pyare."

Mrinu looked at Anjana. She wondered if she knew who she was, if she had made peace with herself.

"My real name is Akanksha. It means wish."

Anjana was looking across the distance. It was almost time for evening prayers. The sun was setting, and the light softened her features; the lines around her eyes were less pronounced, her jaw more rounded. For a few seconds Anjana looked as Mrinu thought she might want to be seen.

The spell was broken as soon as Anjana felt the attention. She played to it, flicking her hair. "Don't be such a drama queen! It's not going to be easy, you know. There were people here, building up your identity for you, Mrinamayi, Akanksha, Sheila – other people made you who you are. You'll have to decide who you want to be now. I don't think you just find out or discover it, I really don't. You will have to decide."

"Really?"

"When I was dumped by my family, I was picked up by people who knew, who had decided for me. They told me who I was. Look at me. I am not an accident. I am a product

83

of what they wanted for me. I'm not one of a kind, I'm one of thousands, with our clothes and the way we talk and the songs we sing. You need to decide who you want to be now. It won't be easy, my love. Not one bit."

Mrinu and Anjana walked on in silence. They picked out their baskets of offerings for Ma Kali and offered their prayers in the tiny room. They were the only people there today. There was no need to queue or pay extra for the VIP line. The priest looked them over and it seemed he might turn Anjana away, but then he shrugged and said nothing.

Anjana and Mrinu moved on, not daring to stay longer than required. They found a small tea stall and perched on the floor, away from the glares or curious looks of the population that parted and merged like flood water on the pavements. Anjana lit a bidi and Mrinu inhaled the second-hand smoke. Somewhere a bell was being rung, a tram rattled along the road and Mrinu wondered if she would ever bother coming back again.

As if reading her thoughts, Anjana took her hand.

"Carry this with you always."

Not quite understanding what she meant, Mrinu looked questioningly at her friend.

"This," she signalled, waving her hand across the scene before them. "A customer once said that we must always take pictures, if not with a camera, then with our minds, that way we will never forget."

"That's a very wise thing to say."

"He read a lot," nodded Anjana. "One day, all this will

seem like another person's life, as if a close friend related the events to you one day. It won't seem real. But you won't forget. And you mustn't. This is a part of you, the strong part, the part that made you want to change things."

Mrinu nodded this time. Her eyes, moist with tears. She wiped them away with the end of her sari, smudging the kohl slightly, that rimmed her eyes.

13

1981. Monsoon, Calcutta, India

Akanksha changed silently in the dark of her bedroom. She wore the jeans and the kurti she occasionally wore when she met Subhash. She wrapped her hair into a tight bun and, carrying her sandals and her handbag, went down the stairs. With every step she asked God to keep her from falling or tripping. Please, please, please, she whispered with every footfall. When she reached the bottom, she mouthed a word of thanks. The front door would be trickier. She opened the door noiselessly but prepared for the deep thud and tight click it would make as she closed it behind her. Outside, the rain fell with heavy rhythmic drips. She did not bring an umbrella and she cursed her stupidity. She moved quickly, every step taking her further and further away. She did not look back, half expecting to be chased.

Her heart was pounding and suddenly she was alive. The rain seemed to cleanse her as she realised she was drenched, hair dripping, clothes saturated. It was as if she had bathed in the Ganges itself. She stood still for a moment and felt her blood rushing, she was aware of every tiny thing around her. Suddenly, she began to run, simply because her energy needed an outlet. Life had moved too slowly in the past.

She reached the auto-rickshaw stand and asked to be taken to Howrah Train Station. She watched the scenery zoom past the open sides and the rain splashed against her face. Akanksha closed her eyes and delighted in the speed the lack of traffic allowed.

Daily routines were causing him to grind his teeth in the night.

Her smiles seemed inane. What on Earth was there to smile about?

They were scraping by, at best.

There was a baby on the way, there was a loan to repay and she had simply stopped getting out of bed. She had hired another maid in the last month, someone new to help with the baby for when it would be born. Although the baby would not come into existence for another three months, Saira insisted that it was essential to have someone with her now at all times. She had no mother to help and Tinku's own mother had, by his own admission, lost her mind.

She would send the maid out and order food from nearby restaurants and then throw most of it away because she just couldn't finish it. Sometimes she would venture out of bed, walk around the flat, then complain of exhaustion. When Tinku arrived home, she would be sleeping, waking just in time for her evening meal in bed. He could not understand her wasteful behaviour. He had also had news recently that his father had gone through with the threat of cutting Tinku out of his will. The money instead would go to his nephew who lived abroad.

Tinku had thought that starting a family was what he wanted but, before even the baby was born, he felt trapped. He could envisage Saira neglecting the child. He could see her demanding more and more for herself, with no thought of the consequences. He considered moving out of this flat and finding somewhere smaller, but dreaded bringing up the topic.

This morning, Saira made the effort to get out of bed. She sighed and put her hand to her head, feeling lightheaded and nauseous. She tried on a smile, a grimace she had been using these days, to make things seem better than they were. She had noticed Tinku pull away and understood why. It was perhaps time to set things right.

She walked out of the bedroom and watched her husband sit down to eat.

Silence.

She stared, willing him to look in her direction, but he avoided her gaze. What had happened to them? They should be happier, they should be excited, they had a baby on the way, but he stalked about the house like a caged animal, his diminutive frame casting huge shadows in the doorways, blocking out the light, making it difficult to breathe. She herself felt lost, bewildered, out of control.

She cleared her throat, searching for something to say. When Tinku finally looked at her in challenge, there were no words. Saira watched him get up, put on his socks and shoes, then wordlessly open the door to leave. She tried to make some move to embrace him, to kiss him goodbye but it was already too late. He had gone.

As if drugged, Saira's head would not clear. In just two hours, her flat turned into something unclean. She gagged. He had given two of the maids a day off today without consulting her. A way to punish her for getting pregnant, she believed. It would mean that she would have to do some of the housework today or watch the mound of household debris rise around her.

She picked up the breakfast dishes and took them to the sink. There were the dishes from the night before piled precariously in the basin, ready to tumble. One dirty plate balanced on another, bits of rice, curry, a forgotten piece of cucumber, a fork, a knife, lots and lots of little spoons. She focused. She would leave the spoons until last. They were the most troublesome. She wondered why the cook had not done them, but then she realized that she had already left, taking advantage of Saira's late rising. A bubble of nausea travelled up through her gut as she caught the residual odour of onions from the chopping board. The full-time maid should have done this last night, but Saira was too tired to tell her.

With this pregnancy everything just smelled stronger. She

retched at the thought of cooking food and washing dirty dishes. It seemed she was literally allergic to the kitchen. She would have to order the food from the restaurant and hope they deliver.

After washing up she opened her diary. She had kept one since she was young. These days she tried to fill the pages with something positive; she thought it would be good for the baby. There was nothing positive in her head. She closed the diary and picked up a book of Hindu baby names. Ones she had previously liked seemed uninspired now. She put the book away, and caught sight of her reflection in the mirror. Dark circles, wild hair and cracked lips frowned back at her.

I need a shower, she thought. After that, she would go out, she would take a yellow taxi down to the river, watch the boats and the sadhus and the women who bathed without heed and washed without care their bodies and their clothes. She might even buy some puchkas, her favourite street food, savouring the tang of spices, trying to hold the liquid in her mouth without it dribbling down her chin.

Perhaps it was time to start going out again.

⸙

He looked at the phone on his desk. Colleagues came out from their team meetings and chatted idly before starting again.

"Gosh! That was a long one!"

"Hmm," he replied distractedly.

He shouldn't have left the house that way. The finances

would work themselves out. She couldn't be happy if she was behaving this way, her smiles weren't real. He played back the breakfast scene in his mind.

He left the room, muttering 'cigarette break', and took the lift. He hadn't smoked in a while, but he was craving one now. After just half a cigarette he began to feel lightheaded. He rang Saira's phone from the STD-PCO shop across the road from the office but there was no answer. He stubbed out the cigarette under his foot and walked back inside. It was dark after the sunlight and it took some time for his eyes to adjust. He walked to his desk and resumed his work.

It was lunch time before he thought to call again and again there was no answer.

Perhaps she was angry with him. He would get some flowers on the way home. They'd talk things through.

Later that evening, he got into his car and turned on the ignition. A bunch flowers was on the passenger seat and there were flowers for her hair; one day she said she would like to wear them again. He had spoken to his boss and would apply for the team leader post that had come up, and he was pretty much guaranteed to get it. Things were looking up; they'd get through this; they were going to be a family. A year from now he'd be settled into his role as a father, his Saira would be a wonderful mother, and they all would be content.

Tinku Majumdar, good name Tarun, was about to get into his car when a colleague, sweating and out of breath, called his name. There was a phone call for him. He could take it in reception.

"Hello?" Tinku said.

"Good afternoon, is this Mr Majumdar?"

"Yes, Can I help you?"

"I'm Police Inspector Dey. I'm sorry to have to inform you but we believe that your wife met with an accident this morning. She was rushed to hospital and all attempts were made to resuscitate her. In the end, I'm afraid they were unsuccessful. We will need you to come to the hospital to identify the body."

He listened, responded to the questions, and put the phone down. He walked out into the evening where life continued. The lights were coming on and the street sellers began to set up their stalls afresh.

He got into the car filled with the overpowering perfume of flowers.

Tinku Majumdar vomited onto the parking lot floor.

A crow came and landed a few feet away, watching curiously, waiting for the man and the car to move off to some other business.

PART THREE

Daughters

14

2002. Autumn, Nuneaton, England

"Slowly, slowly now."

Shika heard the voice from far away. She was on the floor of their living room, propped up against Mark. What was she doing there, what had happened?

"You fainted," said her son, Max, as if he knew what she asked.

"Baba? Was it a dream?"

"No. He passed away this afternoon."

Fresh tears fell on her cheeks. Her father had been the constant. He never left her; she left him.

"Ma?"

"Your mother is at the hospital, Shik. Shall we go? Do you think you can?"

"I have to. Do the others know?"

"I've managed to get a hold of all of them. They're on their way here. Tara can stay here to let them in."

"Tara needs to be there." Her father, in the last few months of his life had begun to dote on his granddaughter as he doted on his first daughter with the same name. Occasionally, when he was in a lot of pain, he would ask Tara to sing a song that his daughter had known, and Tara could not oblige him. He would cry then.

"No matter," he would eventually say, "just hold my hand until I fall asleep."

Earlier that year, Shika had lost Bella. Cancer had crawled into her body, settled in the darkness and eaten away at the life that had not yet had enough of living. It felt as if they were still mourning her. She thought of her mother again, ever-resilient against the relentless onslaught of grief she was forced to face again and again.

They left a key with the neighbour as they squeezed into the car that had always been too small. Today it felt huge. She sat in the front passenger seat, isolated; Max too was on his own in the corner, where he always liked to be, huddled as far away from the rest of the world as he could be; even Tara, normally the one to take up space with her gestures and enthusiasm, remained still. Her husband, Mark, was helpless against the grief. He held on tightly to the steering wheel, staring through the endless rain. What did he know about death?

Two deaths now. With every passing, Shika lost a little of herself. He wondered at the way she watched her sister die and yet continued to be his wife, his children's mother, her parents' daughter. Her depression disappeared, strangely enough, as if her mind had said: this, now is true sadness. Why on Earth, were you sad before?

They reached the hospital. The rain had stopped falling, the clouds had cleared, the sun was going down. The sky was orange, red, blue, yellow, purple and pink. When Tara was very young they would name and count the different hues whenever they saw such a sky.

As they stepped out of the car, Shika remembered the letter in the kitchen, the reason her mother had left them all, the smell of Horlicks that still made her gag. She would have to wait to tell her husband, after the children had gone to bed. She needed to talk to her mother first. She never told her sister about her father's infidelity, she had to believe she had done the right thing. There was nothing to be gained from such knowledge, there was only a burden to be carried, never to be set down.

Through the main entrance, down the corridor on the left, turn right, take the lift, through another corridor. A maze she had mastered, first with the birth of her children, then with the death of her sister. She knew the cafeteria and the gift shops, she knew cleaners and the nurses, and they seemed to know her. It was strange, she thought, only the doctors seemed to have moved on.

She found the room even before they had the chance to tell her they had moved him. The sight of him winded her, and bile rose in her throat. She held her daughter's hand tightly. Her mother's head was on her father's chest which was not rising and falling in giant breaths, but motionless.

This was not her father. She would not touch him. This was a body.

Shika ached from sitting up next to her mother's bed. Mamta's fever had finally broken, and she was now sleeping peacefully. Her bed and her clothes were soaked however and Shika knew she needed to wake her to change the bed. Her mother was not a small woman. The weight gain around her middle was gradual and eventually dangerous. She had been diagnosed with diabetes and the pills she had taken to control the condition had stopped working long ago.

Shika and Mark had finally persuaded her to move in with them, and despite the initial teething problems it had worked out well. Shika could not imagine what she would have done if her mother had been alone when she suddenly fainted. Her fever had lasted two days and two nights – a possible urine infection, the doctor thought. He said that at this age, her mother would be prone to all kinds of complications due to her diabetes.

Shika wondered if it was wise to broach the issue that eaten at her since her father's death. Mamta had not mentioned her father's affair since she returned all those years ago and Shika sometimes thought she had dreamt it all.

Slowly, quietly, close to her mother's ear, Shika whispered for her mother to wake up. Mamta's eyelids fluttered and then she jerked herself awake.

"I was dreaming of your father. He was a ghost. He was

telling me that he was coming to take me with him. I told him I did not want to go."

"It was a dream, Ma. Come, let's get you something dry and clean to wear and some food. Your sugar levels must be very low."

The old woman complied. She looked like a vulnerable, scared child, and was shaking as Shika supported her towards her own bedroom.

Mark was already downstairs, making tea for them all. It was Sunday morning, usually his day to lie in, but he had thought better of it and got out of bed early when he realised his wife had not come to bed for the second night in a row. He did not worry about her as much any more. He could hear the stirrings coming from upstairs and he poured another cup of tea for his mother-in-law. Ma, he called her. She would have none of this first name nonsense that the English people did with their elders. She tried to talk to him in English, but mostly she spoke through Shika, telling him how she did not approve of this or that. Sometimes she complained that her daughter was too strict and occasionally she smiled broadly at him when he smuggled her some vanilla ice-cream. She complained that her grandchildren could not respond to her in her own tongue, but often asked Max to just sit next to her as they shared the one passion they had in common, watching Sachin Tendulkar play; and she had taught Tara how to knit, without words, but by taking the needles and making her watch, as she unstitched and stitched. Together, they made a scarf, uneven, full of holes and of as many different colours they could manage. As soon as it was cold enough, Tara would wear the scarf to school. She wore it every day until one day even Tara became aware of the musty dullness it had taken on from not being washed.

Mamta would sit by the window whenever she came down and watching passers-by through the criss-cross lattice. The mismatched, nameless couple and their dogs, Brian the elderly yet energetic walker, the children to and from school, balancing on walls, or racing ahead. And when she grew tired of the reality, the sameness, the muted greys and blues, she would turn her attention to the drama and colour on the small screen that she insisted be on all the time. Sometimes, Shika would join her, but most of the time she watched alone. Mark did not have the patience for such things. He balked at the over-acting, the murders and the mysticism.

"How could one watch such tripe?" he would remark, more than once.

"It's no different to the karate and gun-fights you enjoy watching, with men and their superhuman strength and fast cars and half naked women," Shika would respond.

When Mamta escaped into these worlds, she no longer remembered herself. She would lean in closer to the small screen, her chin resting on her fist, arm propped up by her leg balanced on a footstool. Sometimes when someone would call her, she would not hear them until they tapped her on her shoulder, as if waking her from a dream.

Some days when Shika was in the kitchen chopping vegetables, grinding poppy seeds, marinating meat, Mamta would come and join her. She would find a plastic plate and the knife that did not cut so well and tell of the time when she used to cut vegetables on the floor, with a type of cutlass. It was called a Boti Daa and was sharpened regularly with a stone. It rested on the floor and women would bend over it, holding the stand steady with one foot as the used both hands to guide the vegetable against the blade. With it, one could slice a potato as thinly as a slice of moon. But, she would always add, before she was married no one had taught her to chop and slice and cook. It was Shika's cousin who had taught Mamta to cook. He would always be by her side, just a boy, with a little bit of fluff above his lip and at odd places on his cheeks and chin. He showed her everything she knew, from how to remove the bitterness from the gourd by soaking it in salt water to the correct way of balancing a kadai on a flame. She said he did all this because Mamta was the only one who treated him kindly, in spite of the effeminate ways that others did not like.

When Tara came home wanting a nose-pin, Mamta told of the day she gave birth to Chotu, writhing in agony, drenched in sweat, slipping in and out of consciousness until the child was born. It was at that time she stopped wearing a nose-pin because the one she had, of a golden 'S', had slipped out, never to be found again. She dared not ask her husband for another, not when money was tight and times were hard.

These stories she told again and again, but she never mentioned her sadness and pain when she was taken to a land where she shivered with loneliness and cold, she never spoke of the betrayal and the losses and the pain.

"How could I bring it all up now?" Shika asked herself. Now her mother seemed small, withered and worn, like a leaf in autumn, her hair had turned white and wrinkles appeared; before Baba's death her skin was as smooth as a ripe apple and her hair was dark as night. Somehow, when he died he had taken with him, something of Mamta. There was nothing left to rebel against, nothing left to be angry at.

15

2002. Winter, Nuneaton, England

"The village is called Sonarpur. It is just outside Calcutta. The woman's name was Ambika Devi. I believe she works as a maid in other people's houses, although she'll be too old for that now. She had a daughter and that is all I know."

"Thank you, Ma."

Her mother continued watching the street. Daylight was fading now; the streetlights were coming on. Soon, they would have to turn on the lights in the living room and draw the curtains to stop others from seeing in. Mamta hated the winter for this. She did not want to look into her daughter's eyes, and instead struggled to stand up. Shika moved out of her way.

"I will be in my room, chanting God's name. Put the light on in the Puja room and call me down when Mark gets home. You will need to speak to him if you want to go on this silly mission of yours."

Shika had predicted this reaction. She was nearly fifty years old and yet her mother still made her feel like a silly, incompetent child. Shika needed to do this and knew Mark would support her. The children were old enough to take care of themselves and they would have their father and their grandmother.

She longed for Max to come home. Her boy, who made her smile just by the smile on his own face, the dimple on his cheek, the extravagant hugs, arms wrapped tightly around her neck. At fourteen he was taller than her now, and as skinny as a rake, all elbows and knees. His hair, curly until he was about four, was straight and his eyes were becoming lighter. He had started to resemble his father until one day their shadows almost matched. But Max had a way of making light of a situation by just being. Perhaps he consumed the darkness and turned it into something else, something brighter and happier. Tara could not do this. Tara brooded a lot, was angered and cried often, and took life too seriously. She would take the darkness and make it darker in an attempt to vanquish it. She would then be left exhausted. She was a child of extremes: studying so hard, she would forget to eat and sometimes, laughing so hard that she would collapse on the floor sobbing. Sometimes her mother worried for her sanity. She demanded attention, it was essential they told her they loved her, or she was convinced they did not. She would berate herself and scratch her own face with her nails, leaving red lines. Tara was just like Bella, thought Shika.

The computer was up in the attic bedroom. Shika had

forgotten the password to the laptop so she made her way to the second floor, passing her mother's bedroom on the way. She could hear the ancient Walkman, buzzing with the song that held all of the Goddess' one hundred and eight names. Her mother's shrill voice, slightly off key and slightly out of time echoed the names one by one: Bhavani, Durga, Tara, Sati, Parvati, Cinta and on and so on.

As she walked through her son's room to reach the stairs to the attic, she picked up his pyjamas and the book he was reading the night before and placed them neatly on the bed. She would have to talk to him about tidying his room, she thought.

Up in the attic, where they carried out their daily worship, the room smelled of burning oil and incense. The flowers from the morning Puja had already wilted and would be removed by Shika's mother in a little while. It was normally Shika who carried out this duty, putting the Goddess to sleep when the sun went down, but while she was menstruating she was not deemed clean enough. The old woman then had to perform the ritual. Mark did not understand, and nor did he want to. He would be home soon, thought Shika as she stopped to kneel at the little shrine.

She looked at the Goddess's face and prayed silently for strength and resolve, for the wisdom to choose between what was right and what was wrong. She prayed for the anger she held still towards her mother to be lessened; she prayed that the Goddess keep her family safe. She touched her forehead to the ground and thanked the Goddess for all that she had been given and then stood up, making sure she had disturbed nothing.

As Shika waited for the monitor to come on, she flicked through the photographs in the desk drawer. They were in unsealed envelopes, marking the important days, festival days, days when relatives had come to visit, days when the children were still children, toddling, crawling, slurping ice-cream. The monitor waited for Shika now, as she toyed with the idea of just giving up on the idea of finding a half-sister who she was not even sure existed. She turned off the screen and continued to look through the photographs.

The room became dark as the light faded outside, and Shika did not notice her son come in, padding softly on the laminate flooring. His coat was still on, over the top of a blazer that was getting a little too small. He hugged her from behind, startling her and forcing her to drop the photographs. Max turned on the light and knelt down, picking up the photograph closest to his own foot. It was of his mother and her sister, shortly after he was born. He was there in his aunt's arms, cradled and safe. Words did not need to be uttered. Max helped his mother up and held her tightly, like he knew she liked. She gave way to the grief she had held on to for so long.

Later that evening, Shika told Max and Mark about her father and her half-sister. She told them what she wanted to do and how she needed to do it. They nodded and told her they understood. They would tell Tara at the weekend, when she would be home and relaxed, too tired to be angry. Shika cried a little more and then went upstairs to find her mother. She was sitting on her bed, stroking Baba's shawl.

"I wanted you to hate him. You always loved him without question. You never saw how he hurt me, you never seemed to care."

"I did care, Ma. But I did not want my family to break. I was just a child. What could I have done?"

"I had no one to fight for me. Your father had set up a life for us where I was expected to just slot in and make do. When we arrived on the plane, your brothers, you and your sister, I had to handle you all, by myself. You cried the whole time and complained of earache, Chotu was scared and the others would not sit still. There was one elderly gentleman, also a Bengali, who saw me struggling. He helped me ask the stewardess for some milk for Chotu. I was so grateful, I cried. I did not see him again. If I wanted to find anyone, I would search for him. I would not search for someone who stole your father from me."

"I'm not doing this to hurt you, Ma. I need to find her. I need to know whether she looks like Baba or like Bella or like me, or nothing like any one of us. She's a part of Baba and he's gone. Perhaps she would like to know."

"You do what you have to do. I'll be here when you get back."

"I'll book my tickets tomorrow." Shika tried to hug her mother but received no response. Her mother sat like a rock.

Shika felt the anger swelling inside her, the anger that she had quelled a long time ago. She had not forgiven her mother and she had not forgiven her father.

Breathe, she told herself. Breathe and concentrate on the rise and fall of your chest. Close your eyes and picture nothingness. She could feel the weight lifting, the knot in her stomach untwisting.

Shika packed a small suitcase with things she thought she may need such as toiletries and sanitary towels, things she believed she would not be able to find in Calcutta – Kolkata, not Calcutta. She had booked herself into a hotel and had left detailed instructions for her children. Her mother was barely talking to her. Shika wondered if this silence would end and assumed it would, eventually, but after she returned. Mark watched amused as Shika attempted to pack. Her mound of clothes was reaching a peak at the centre of the case. He waited until she left the room and then repacked so they laid flat and were evenly distributed throughout the case. When Shika returned she smiled gratefully.

"I wish you could come too."

"I won't get time off work."

"I know. Look after yourself and don't work too late. Remember Ma and Max will be waiting for you. Perhaps Tara could come home for a week to keep Ma company during the day."

"Don't worry, I'll try to wangle it so I can work from home some days. And on the days I can't, I'll take her to one of the strange aunties' houses."

Shika looked at Mark, who was, in turn looking at himself

in the mirror, adjusting his hair and wondering whether he could leave it another week before he had it cut again. Unchanged and unwavering, he was always on her side. Somewhere the love still grew, without disturbing anything else around it; silently it would rest, curled up between them, warming them, until they had become so accustomed to its presence they would not be able to sleep if it were absent.

She came up behind him and took his hand.

"You can do this, but you don't have to. You can still decide not to go."

"I need to."

"Is it really that important?"

"Yes."

"Then be strong."

Her flight was in the evening. She was troubled by the fact that she had not spoken properly to Tara, who had not come home from university at the weekend, as it was her housemate's birthday party; the phone conversations were perfunctory.

Shika went downstairs. Max was in the living room, taking advantage of the fact that his grandmother had not yet taken control of the television for the day. He was watching cars zoom around on a track, impossibly fast. The crowds were watching, standing at the very edge, exhilarated by the speed, noise and possible danger. Shika thought it ironic that her son, usually so slow and methodical, could find pleasure in such a sport. Perhaps that was the attraction, knowing that this was something that he would never be.

She picked up the cordless phone in the kitchen, and dialled her daughter's mobile number and waited for the click and the answer. None came. She hung up and tried again. This time, a man's voice answered.

"Hello, is this Tara's phone?"

"Yeah, who's this?"

"Sorry, who are you?" Shika was confused. How had this man picked up her daughter's phone?

"Hold on." There was a pause before Tara came on the line.

"Hi, Ma. I've been meaning to talk to you, but it just never seemed quite the right time."

Shika decided to ignore it for the time being and pretend the implications did not exist.

"I need to tell you something, first. I wanted to tell you face to face, this weekend but you did not come home."

There was a long pause on the other end.

"Hello?"

"What is it?"

Shika related all that she could across a telephone line. She wanted to hold her hand as she told her about the husband who was unfaithful, about the grandfather who was not so pure, but she had to make do with waiting, just waiting for the reaction to come. It did not come, at least not one that she had expected.

"I'll come home in a couple of days. I'll stay with Nani while you're gone. You're doing the right thing. I think I would have done the same."

Later on, as Shika assessed her luggage, she thought about how her children had begun to take on the responsibility of taking care of her needs. She had not asked them, but somehow they did, just as she had done for her parents and her siblings. She felt a jolt of pride. She was ready to leave.

Mark took her to the airport. The security bag check, checking in her suitcase, going through the metal detectors, all seemed unreal. They held no significance towards the journey she was taking, the task she was undertaking.

She thought about her sister Bella, the one who always rebelled, who wanted to run away but always ended up pulling everyone towards her. She was like a flame who had burned too brightly and like a strip of magnesium, she had burnt herself out. Her reaction would have been to scream and shout and yelp and blame, but her anger would have come and gone. It would not have poisoned her, as it had poisoned Shika, who trusted no one; even as she married Mark there was a part of her who was waiting for him to leave. Her own children she had let go, taking note of every sign that they would not stay with her for long. But they had all proved her wrong. How much time had she wasted on suspicion and mistrust?

The journey was uneventful, the food was bland and too hot. She remembered what her mother had briefly told her about her own aeroplane journey, towards another life with three children to manage: two boys, two girls, and the ghost of another. Then the trust her mother placed in her husband had been shattered.

Shika tried the movies on the tiny monitor on the back of the seat in front. She scrolled through the channels with the touch screen that sometimes moved too quickly or not quickly enough. She stopped when she came to something with that blonde actress with the big smile and the man with floppy hair and English accent. She often could not remember their names, but their faces signalled a romantic comedy. It was not something that she could usually watch with Mark, so she took the opportunity now, for the first time, enjoying the fact that she was without him or anyone else. Her eyelids soon closed, too heavy with the effort of focusing. The other passengers had also given up for the day. The lights had been dimmed, the baby who had been crying throughout, had finally quietened and there was nothing else keeping Shika awake. She gave into the sleep that finally came.

16

2002. Winter, Calcutta, India

It was the heat that hit Shika first, then the smell, and finally the noise. She was suddenly aware of the fact that she was sweating, drips snaking down her back, leaving stains under her arms. It was supposed to be winter. November, after the Puja, was when the climate was miraculously perfect in the city, she was told. The perfect time to visit. She was not ready for this heat though, nor the onslaught of people begging, demanding and pushing her to spare a few coins or slide into the back of their cab.

One man stood out. He was taller than the others and it was he who led her to a taxi within the long line of cars that looked like overgrown canaries. He snatched her case from her hands and bundled it into the trunk. Again, she asked herself, what she was doing here. An impulse to get out of the taxi, walk back to the airport and board a plane home was slowly taking over her ability to think of anything else.

The taxi driver asked her where she was going in a Hindi, all throaty consonants and disguised vowels so unlike the movies, she took time to grasp. She gave him the name of a hotel she believed was near the centre of the city and he grunted in recognition.

The ride was a stop and start journey, rarely moving faster than thirty kilometres an hour. The open windows let in the dust and the sun. There were men urinating on the side of the road every few hundred yards; there were shacks selling packets and pots of things and shacks that seemed to hold contraptions for juicing just about everything; there were women, with babies balanced on their hips, begging; children were begging too, their matted hair bleached by the sun; there were white-uniformed officials in dark glasses; there were men and women on scooters and motorbikes, handkerchiefs covering their mouths and noses as they waited and moved. And just as Shika could not help but look, it seemed that all eyes were on her, assessing her, building a story in their heads about who she might be. Sometimes there would be a knock on the window, women, children, men with missing limbs and the other kind, neither men or women but between, all asking her for the money they were sure she had. Shika refused to give, knowing from what she had been told that if she gave to one, she would have to give to them all. The last time she was here, she was getting married. Nothing had changed.

Eventually she arrived at the hotel. She looked at the meter and saw a number that was lower than expected.

"Kotho hoiche? How much?" She asked, stuttering.

The taxi driver produced a card, pointed to the meter and read out the corresponding number, something more appropriate for the length of the journey. Should she tip? Shika decided against it. She had never been here alone; she was always the dependent. The taxi driver pulled out Shika's bag and left it on the pavement outside the hotel entrance. A man at the front of the hotel, turbaned and regal, touched a gloved hand to his head, nodding slightly in greeting. She was signalled to put her case and bag through an x-ray machine, like they had at the security check at the airport; she felt as if she had already done something wrong. She entered and walked to the front desk. The air conditioning provided her with the relief she craved. Thirty-one degrees, they said, was the outside temperature. Too hot for England and the English. Too hot for Shika.

The interiors were modern, sleek and black with not a speck of dirt. A giant aquarium with gigantic fish of blue, orange, purple and gold took up the whole of the front desk. Whilst bubbles floated at waist height, Shika checked in and handed over her passport and credit card for verification.

She was finally handed the key, a card that would allow her into her room. A bellboy, dressed in a shabby uniform followed her up with her case and helped her enter as she fumbled with the card. She tipped him and he left smiling, thanking her. The card was placed in a holder which, in turn controlled the light switch, Shika experimented and found the card had to remain in the holder for the lights or any of the electrics to work.

115

She suddenly remembered her phone in her handbag. She had not looked at it since she was on the plane. She took it out now. There was a tiny amount of battery left. She hoped it would be enough to make a quick call home, to let them know she had arrived. No one answered. She tried again and this time it was picked up straight away. It was her mother, her voice gruff, unrecognisable at first, almost like a man's.

Closing her eyes, she let her mouth say the words she needed to.

"I've arrived safely. Remember to take your medicines on time. I'll call later."

The phone was disconnected and Shika decided to sleep first and shower later. Food was the last thing on her mind.

Shika looked at the name written in a hurried hand with black ink smudged and untidy in her diary. She touched the letters, wondering about the other woman who lay with her father. Time had softened her feelings towards her, and she knew she may not be the villainess Shika had painted her to be. Hopefully she would be able to find the address written below the name if she went by taxi. Her broken Bengali caused her to stumble over words and make her look unsure of what she was doing. She stood out, as a tourist, despite the fact she looked like the other Calcuttians on the street, trying hard to blend in with her salwar kameez and pony tailed hair.

She looked at the other names in the diary. One was that of her cousin, a much older man, capable, married and from the little interaction she had had with him, principled and stern. She knew he would help her; she also felt he might judge her. Somehow she felt he would not understand what it was she wanted to do. There was no logical reason to look for her father's mistress and their child. Even as Shika said it out aloud it made no sense, but she needed someone. She would call him, she decided.

She finished her breakfast and showered. She picked through the clothes she had brought with her and settled on a green top with some floral bottoms, traditionally cut to make her look… more Indian. When had she changed? When had she become a foreigner in the land where she had spent much of her childhood? Was it the first time she tasted pork sausages or when she married an English man, a physical embodiment of her rejection for what her father had wanted for her? Shika had made it clear that she had chosen her future over her past, to a whole new way of living, of drinking openly if she chose, to eating meat on a Thursday, of learning to make lasagne and spaghetti bolognese in the evenings, instead of boiling rice and soaking lentils and descaling fish. She spoke in English at home except to converse with her mother, making it difficult for Tara to learn her mother tongue. She did not attend the functions and the birthdays of the community she had grown up in, instead she arranged for her mother to be dropped off and picked up from these events. It was a conscious decision to reject, but it was a gradual insidious change that had occurred within her until she was no longer comfortable in her own skin, that skin which made her stand out in her husband's world as well. She was deemed exotic, from another land, Mark's foreign wife. Yet she was more or less content until her father's death. After that, she wondered if there was another version of herself somewhere out there.

Shika dialled the number from the phone in her hotel room. She counted the rings before a man's voice answered from across a distance.

"Hello." An absurd urge, made her want to respond with: "is it me you're looking for?"

She managed to restrain a nervous giggle and berated herself silently before she trusted herself to speak. She explained her situation to her cousin. He explained that if she could wait until this evening, he would meet her and be happy to help. Shika accepted an invitation to his house for dinner. After hanging up the phone, she wondered if she should venture out and do some sightseeing. She had not thought of the moments in between the seeking and finding.

There was not much of a view from the window. She saw a train line and a ramshackle brick building in the distance, wooden shutters worn and weathered by neglect and the elements. She saw a black cat on the winding iron stair well that ran along the side of the hotel. A part of the past clashed with the inside of the ultra-modern hotel room, where she stood and watched. The cat came right up to the window and regarded Shika curiously. It reminded her a little of Tara's cat. She hadn't thought about it in years and yet, just something in the expression of the little creature, its assuredness, brought back a sack full of memories and associations. Despite everything, she felt a twinge of nostalgia for the time when she was happy enough to just deal with the present, the cat and the baby and the little girl and the husband, when the unknown did not niggle at her and nudge her awake when she slept.

She decided against stepping out and explored the television instead. She found it to be soothing, lighting up the quiet with familiar American faces that she had seen a hundred times. She did not know when she fell asleep but when she awoke, it was already dark. The television was still on and Shika scrabbled around the bed and covers for the remote control. She found the power button and turned the room black unexpectedly. She hated the darkness; it made her feel claustrophobic and scared. Memories of nightmares after Tara her sister had died suddenly landed in the room with her. She had never known her, but the story filled her own childhood nights with dread. What if death came for all the little girls in her family? She turned the television back on, needing the voices to create the illusion of company.

She re-combed her hair and washed her face, willing the sleepiness away with the salty tepid water from the tap. The bathroom suddenly felt hot after the air-conditioned coolness of the bedroom and Shika rushed out and took in the cold blast of relief from the bedroom. She stood still for a time, aware that she was alone. It was a rare feeling.

She found her bag and her shoes and wondered about mosquito repellent. She decided she would not bother

119

tonight, as she would travel in a taxi to someone's home, unlikely to be troubled by biting insects.

In the lobby tacky decorations of gold, red and green adorned every nook. She saw guests arriving with their suitcases, as she had done the previous day, and she wondered whether there was anyone else who had a similar purpose to hers. Then she stepped out into the streets. All she saw were people. Rich people with their designer shopping bags, poor people with their begging bowls, and all people in between, just going about their lives.

A tram rattled passed and Shika stared at the rickety contraption, yellow, rusted and barely holding itself together as people leant out, ready to jump off. The lights from the shops invited her in, promised her sanity and, whilst outside, right in front of her was the staggering population, rushing past, focused and uncaring. Just once she caught a glimpse of another woman with the same expression as herself. She was white, dressed like a hippy and had probably come to India to find enlightenment. Shika pondered what she had found in Calcutta. What spirituality could be gleaned from the depths of this darkness?

Yellow cabs rumbled past and she watched the locals hailing them. It seemed simple. She just needed to catch the driver's attention and hold out her hand. She was successful in her first attempt. A ripple of pride shot through her and she gave the address of her cousin's house with an unexpected confidence.

This ride was better than the last; there was not so much standing still in traffic this time. The air was cooler and less dusty so Shika did not feel the pollution filling her lungs as she had previously. She did, however, regret her decision not to wear mosquito repellent. Her arms and feet felt tiny pin pricks of pain, signalling that she had become a feeding vat. A part of her wondered about malaria and she thought about what she would do if she were to fall ill. She did not have the sturdiest of constitutions and it usually was her who fell prey to any diseases that were floating in the atmosphere. Again, panic set in, until she reminded herself that she was only here for a week and she had a few numbers to call in an emergency, she would be okay. It was like a silent mantra throughout the hour-long journey. The taxi driver tried to coax her into a conversation but Shika would not oblige him. Her replies, if any, were monosyllabic. She clutched her bag close to her, occasionally peeking at her phone and wondering if it would be wise to call Mark. Then she remembered the international calling charges and decided against it. In a few minutes she would be at her cousin's house.

17

2002. Winter, Calcutta, India

Shika looked at her cousin and smiled broadly. It was a comfort that he had not changed. The receding hairline, the thick black moustache, the smiling eyes, the homilies he liked to spin at every turn, all made him seem like a caricature of goodness. His wife had put on weight and was almost unrecognisable, were it not for the fact that as she squeezed Shika, she chided her, calling her Shiku, which only she had dared to do. She was the kind of woman who was intimidated by no one and would offer up her affection to whoever crossed her path. She was uninterested in whether they accepted it or not, she was only concerned with the giving.

Their home had walls of green and pink and orange, where they hung abstract paintings, and on the sound system played ghazals; a man with a voice of velvet and sand sang of love, intoxication, and loss. Shika took off her shoes and left them outside the door, aware of the spotless floors and the maid who was wiping them; she was on her haunches, making wide arcs with a cloth which she occasionally dipped in a bucket of darkening water.

Shika wanted to apologise for disturbing their domesticity, with what she was about to tell them. Pritham Da, she was sure, would be scandalised, his wife would be worldly wise, making a joke that would be meant to be taken for more than face value, a message, a moral for Shika to chew over.

At dinner, Pritham Da ate only two chapattis and some vegetables sautéed in a blend of mild spices, whereas a feast was laid out for Shika and his wife: lentils, fried potatoes and two different dishes of fish, goat and chicken which would be followed by a sweet and sour tomato chutney and sweetened curd. Shika eyed the plates and bowls with apprehension. She knew that she would not be able to do justice to all of the items on display and yet to turn down a single dish would be to offend Boudi, who had painstakingly cooked each item herself. During the meal, Pritham Da ensured he chewed every mouthful exactly eighty times to aid digestion, and exactly twenty minutes after his meal he drank a glass of lukewarm water. His wife had no such patience and gulped down her rice and curries, most of the time talking, asking after the children, Mark, and Shika's mother. Now and then she would be quiet and during those moments Pritham Da would say something serious, thought-provoking or philosophical and Boudi would watch and listen fondly, eyebrows knitted together, mouth closed. Then she would begin again, standing up suddenly to remove a plate or to add some rice or to answer the phone - the phone rang many times during their meal, mostly calls from family members who had heard Shika was in Calcutta. Boudi wisely told them Shika was eating and that she was very tired, assuring them that Shika would get in touch with them as soon as she could but was here on business, for only a few days and, of course, they knew how it was, sometimes there just may not be the opportunity or ease to make the phone call they hoped for.

It was comforting to be there, with them. The family that she had neglected or chosen to forget had refused to let her go. They clung on to her, forcing her to feel a part of their family portrait.

After dinner they brought out the family albums. Pictures of Shika, stick thin and ghostly pale amidst her dark-skinned relatives, pictures of her father with his brothers and his wife, her father's mother who, she noticed, was also fair skinned, the only other person in the photographs who looked like she had been dipped in flour; unnaturally white in a monochrome image of black and greys. She accepted that this was how she inherited her complexion, sought out by many but reviled by Shika herself.

Eventually the time came for Shika to tell Pritham Da and Boudi the truth about why she was here. They knew about her father's death, but this was the first they had heard about the lovechild and the mistress. Pritham Da's initial reaction was to light up a cigarette and inhale deeply. He did not look at Shika. Boudi was also left with nothing to say. But she studied Shika's face, as if looking for a clue to a fitting response. There seemed nothing left to do except apologise, and eventually that was enough for both Boudi and Pritham Da to offer their help in any way they could.

"I hoped you would say that. I need someone to come with me to that woman's house," Shika said.

Pritham Da looked at the address that lay scrawled in Shika's diary. He calculated that it would take about an hour and a half to make the journey, depending on the time of day they left, the conditions of the roads, and whether any special visitors were due in the city. He offered to come with her but pointed out that he would not be able to take leave from his work. Boudi must travel with her, he decided and Boudi agreed, pointing out that Pritham Da would be absolutely fine without her for a day or so.

They discussed how Shika must have felt all these years. They wondered out loud how they had not heard about Shika's mother coming to India all those years ago, they assured Shika that none of what had happened was Shika's fault and then they told her that all of this did not make her father a bad person. She remained emotionless and objective as she spoke about everything that had happened, yet she finally could not keep up the façade any longer. Her face crumpled like a piece of discarded paper and she let out a howl filled with pain. They stroked her hand, patted her back, smoothed the hair away from her face until she cried herself to sleep on their sofa.

Shika did not wake until a shaft of morning light rested on her eyelids. She struggled to remember where or when she was until she recognised the painting on the wall opposite her. Seemingly random splashes of colour on a canvas too large for the space added even more colour to the room that already held too much. She closed her eyes again, letting the colours blur and merge before she blocked them out. She pictured a rainbow in a blue sky, Tara in a plastic yellow raincoat and the West Indian carnival float slowly moving passed them. It was a summer's day, the first time Tara had ever seen a rainbow. She was sitting on Mark's shoulders so she could have a better view of the world she was too small to comfortably inhabit and Shika, only just pregnant with Max, had her arm wrapped around Mark's waist.

As memories turned to dreams, she drifted back to sleep, only to be woken by Pritham Da hovering over her with a cup of tea in his hands and a look of concern on his face.

"You were babbling in your sleep, Shika. How are you feeling?"

Shika smiled, mumbling words that she had slept extremely well and was dreaming.

Pritham Da was already ready for work. His wife was still asleep but would be getting up soon. He apologised for Shika spending the night on the sofa, but they did not want to wake her after she fell asleep.

A few moments later the bedroom door opened and Boudi stepped out. The smile was there, no concern on her face, just the offer of more tea and some breakfast. Famished, Shika agreed readily. She entered their guest bathroom, washed her face and stared back at the reflection in the mirror. There was calm in her eyes, a sense of control. She hated the time difference, it was too early in the U.K. to call home and tell Mark of what had happened.

She wolfed down her breakfast and chatted with Boudi who had made it clear that she would be accompanying her to the village as soon as she was ready. They would have to leave soon or they would hit traffic. Boudi emerged from her bedroom and looked at Shika. She shook her head and told her she would have to change. There were some Indian clothes Boudi had grown out of that would fit her somewhere in the flat. Shika wondered if might be easier to go back to the hotel on the way and change quickly.

The women finally left the house by nine and were at the hotel by ten. Shika was able to get changed and back into the waiting taxi by ten-twenty, which meant they were still stuck in traffic at ten-forty-five. Enthusiasm and optimism began to wane for Shika, and Boudi's prattling was beginning to irritate her. Things were moving too slowly, and the dust and noise and heat settled in the cab. Shika's eyes closed at one point. Boudi, too, had stopped talking long ago and now was watching the traffic, intermittently playing a game on her phone with colourful shapes popping and bursting on the screen. She was unbothered by the pace of the journey.

When Shika opened her eyes, they had slowed again. The road had a different, unfinished quality. The taxi bounced, jostling its passengers into corners and against doors. The driver asked Shika for the address again and it was Boudi who replied. He stopped to ask a man who was carrying a couple of tins of water or oil – Shika could not be sure which – one on each end of a stick balanced on his shoulders. It was like something she had seen in documentaries about poverty. The driver looked around to get his bearings and listened attentively as the water carrier pointed and explained. The man's face was wrinkled and worn, his body, the colour of rosewood, exhibited his ribs and his collarbones in an emaciated, sculpted splendour.

The road ran alongside a small stream. Shika wondered whether it would lead to the sacred Ganges. She kept the question to herself, not wanting to sound like a fool. For a brief moment she had forgotten why they were there, but as the driver got back behind the steering wheel, the butterflies inside her began to flutter.

Boudi looked at her companion and guessed what was going through Shika's mind. She took her left hand and unfurled the fingers, smoothed out Shika's palm, and held her hand until the taxi driver told them he could take them no further, the path was too narrow so they would need to go the rest of the way by foot. Paddy fields stretched out on either side of the walkway, which narrowed further until Shika and Boudi were forced to walk in single file. As it widened again they entered a kind of clearing with houses on either side. Women, some with practical loads balanced on their heads, some with semi clad, curious babes at their hips, watched. Children stood still, interrupting their games to stare at the well-dressed strangers who had come to visit them. It seemed to pass in slow motion for Shika, as Boudi, undeterred and oblivious to the sensation they caused by being there, enquired after Ambika Devi.

The villagers pointed ahead and eventually they pointed to a house with a type of cot at the front. A young girl had already emerged from the house to tell them that Dadi would be out in a moment. Then she ran off.

After a while, a woman emerged from the house. She was dressed in white, like Shika's own mother, symbolising she was a widow. Her hair too was white and her face the colour of toffee. Her loose skin hung from her forearms, and the way she wore her sari, in the traditional Bengali style, revealed the shape of her sagging breasts. It was hard to imagine this woman could be the source of enough desire for a man to jeopardise the happiness of his family. She compared her mother's appearance now, made plump from never having to want, to this woman before her.

Her face was still strong though, and despite the wrinkles her features remained sharp, and her eyes were acute enough to discern who it was that had arrived.

"I am Ambika. You look just like my daughter. You look just like him."

"He's dead." Shika did not know what else to say. She did not know what she was expecting, what she would gain from being here.

"I know. I felt him go about a year ago."

Shika shook her head. It seemed this woman was trying to claim some sort of supernatural emotional tie to her father, as if she were negating Shika and her mother.

129

"How could you know? Do you know how much pain you caused us?"

"I can only imagine, my child. But can you imagine how it was to always be waiting? To know that what was yours could never be claimed? We have had our own sorrows through all of this mess."

Boudi stood and watched. She whispered something into Shika's ear and Shika remembered why she was here.

"I want to find your daughter. I want to meet her. We share the same father."

"She is married. I can give you the address of the family she went to."

The old woman got up from the cot and walked inside, hobbling slightly. She came back out and handed Shika an envelope. "This was the last letter I received from her, about ten years ago. I have not received anything since then."

Just then, the little girl they had seen earlier returned carrying a small plastic bag. She ran inside, her energy seeming to make up for the slowing of time that had suddenly occurred everywhere else around them. She emerged again, carrying a tray of pakoras and some tea. She noted that her Dadi's guests had nowhere to sit and presently brought out two woven stools whilst she herself crouched on the floor.

It felt odd, to accept the hospitality of the woman she had hated for much of her adult life, yet she could find no more in her now except pity and curiosity. She sipped the tea and waited for the silence to break.

"When I first found out Akanksha was growing inside me,

you know, I was elated. My parents had died when I was a young girl of about fourteen or fifteen, almost old enough to marry. My sister and her husband raised me. For me, Akanksha was to be the one being on this earth that I could call my own. But I was sent away to an aunt, my sister came with me and when we returned, the baby was hers. I told your father as soon as I could and by then we had ended. I thought I had done the right thing by telling him of his child, I did not choose to think about his other family. There was a part of me that hoped he would leave you all and stay with me, but of course, he could not do that. He was planning on going away. I let him go, although he promised to send money every month for me and the child. I chose not to marry.

"I kept the money in a bank account, on advice from my brother-in-law. We used it to send Akanksha to a school in the city. We told her the truth as soon as she was old enough to understand. I still wanted to be a mother to her. Privately, I could do that. I braided her hair, fed her, sang to her, told her stories. My sister and her husband were good people. They died within a day of each other just after Akanksha's marriage ceremonies were completed. I was left alone."

"How did you and my father meet? Did you have no regard for my mother?"

Ambika frowned with memory. Then she smiled.

"I was in the field, planting the rice paddy with the other girls. Your father's father owned this land and often sent his sons to inspect the property. That day it was the turn of your father. I had seen him before and was secretly in love with

131

him. He was the most handsome of all the brothers. I watched him from the corner of my eye as he watched me, not bothering to hide his stare. I must have been about sixteen or seventeen. They were looking for a groom for me. I was ready in my mind to marry, to have children. I was excited by the attention."

Shika pictured a young girl, younger than her daughter, toiling in the heat, wading in water that reached her calves. She pictured a young man desiring her. Anger swelled and bubbled up against her father. Ambika continued.

"I met his eyes, which I think shocked and pleased him at the same time. He waited until I had finished and then we met. He took me to show me a nest of mynah birds that had fallen from a tree. Their eggs were a beautiful shade of blue, not like the sky, not like the grass but somewhere in between. He told me I was the most beautiful girl he had seen and that he wanted permission to touch me."

Shika felt a familiar nausea returning. She saw the scene play out in her mind, wanting to look away, to focus on something other than the old woman's raspy voice and wistful gaze. Some part of her wanted the woman to stop but she needed to hear it all, to be faced with the truth of the father whom she had idolised as a child, the man whom she believed was beyond reproach until she noticed her mother's tears scarring her face.

Ambika continued, herself unwilling to relinquish the memory.

"I told him we all belonged to him and that he did not

need my permission to take what was his. I wanted him to touch me. We went into a storeroom that was behind our house and I suppose it began there."

She paused, savouring the moment in her mind. A toothless grimace appeared on her face, slicing it in half, making Shika think of a witch.

"He used to come to me when he did not get what he needed from your mother. He used to leave me in the mornings never knowing when I would see him again. He gave me a mynah bird in a golden cage. I called it Moyna and it learnt to say my name. When your father left to go to a foreign land, I tried to release my Moyna, but she would not go. She hopped out a few steps and then hopped back in, calling my name. I found it dead on the floor of her cage one morning. I cried then for all the things I had not allowed myself to cry for before. I was truly was alone then."

Shika felt no sympathy. She had admitted she wanted her father to leave them.

The tea had turned cold. A chill was settling in as the sun moved lower in the sky. Shika looked at her watch and thanked Ambika for her time.

"I don't ask anything for myself, but this is my sister's granddaughter." Ambika signalled to the girl who had served them their tea. "I have nothing now except my pension. Perhaps you could find it in your hearts to thank me in more practical terms, for her."

Shika did not understand at first, but Boudi had. She took out a couple of notes from her purse and handed it to the girl, who touched her feet, quickly wiping the look of confusion from her face.

Back in the taxi, Shika wondered if there was really anything more to be gained from finding Akanksha. The anonymous half-sister was no longer anonymous. She pictured a mirror image, almost her twin, but clad in a sari, her hair long instead of short the way Shika preferred to wear it these days. She imagined her happy, living with a husband, children, a parallel life to hers. She wondered what would be gained from coming into her life, telling her about the life Shika had led with the father Akanksha never knew.

Boudi was asleep as soon as car began to move. Her chest rose and fell in a comforting rhythm. Shika tried to nudge her awake to discuss what had happened but Boudi would not be stirred. She made a quick calculation about the time difference between home and where she was. One ring, two rings and finally her husband's voice travelled through time and space, an embrace from far away. Shika inhaled and soaked in the idea of him. She had no idea how much she missed him until that 'Hello'.

She told him everything. She asked him what he thought. He told her she should do whatever made her happy. There was nothing left for him to say. She was grateful for the sound of his voice. There was no decision to be made, she should just catch the next plane out of there and return home.

Boudi stirred and let out a single snore, jerking herself awake. She giggled at the realisation of what she had done and forced Shika to join her. The driver put the radio on, and the rest of the journey was made lighter as they all sang along to the classics that were playing at the time.

As they pulled up to the hotel Shika thanked her Boudi for all she had done and assured her she would call later tonight. But for now, she thought she had made her decision. She got out, with a coin ready for the beggar who waited and made her way to her room, saying a silent prayer for the ones who mattered most.

18

2002. Winter, Calcutta, India

Shika awoke sweating. Her hotel room was dark. There was a faint smell of dried fish coming from somewhere, and no sound but for a train bellowing through the city.

She had been dreaming of Bella, and guilt pervaded the dream. Again, she asked what she was doing here. She worried about Tara, about her mother – and she was here, chasing a ghost.

On impulse, she dialled her home number, hoping one of the children would pick up. It was Tara's voice on the other end, angry, as usual.

They spoke calmly for a time, about university, about her Mamta's sugar levels, about the weather. No mention of Calcutta and her task there.

Shika finally hung up, relieved. Her family were fine without her. She just needed to meet Akanksha and that would be it, she would fly back the very next day. She tried to go back to sleep, but the sky was already getting lighter, so she lay in bed for a while, waiting for the birds to begin their chirrups and squawks. Then she had a shower, washing off the dreams.

She shivered in just her towel and got dressed quickly, drying her hair with the hairdryer that hung next to the mirror. Checking the time, she saw it was still early. Pritham Da would not arrive for another hour or so, there was enough time for breakfast.

The lobby was lit with yellow lights, giving the impression that it was still dark outside, reminding Shika of the winter mornings back in the U.K. A twinge of nostalgia hit her suddenly. She wanted to be back in the winter of what was her land now. On the ground floor, Shika realised how hungry she was as she took in the smell of the bread and the fruit. Standing in line for rolls and croissants she had the feeling of being watched. A few minutes later, a middle-aged man came and stood next to her.

"You look awfully familiar," he said. His eyes stared into hers.

"I'm sorry, I'm not from here. You must be mistaking me for someone else."

"Oh, don't worry, I know I don't know you, it's just that you look familiar. You could almost have a double."

Shika put the coffee pot down carefully. She turned to face the man, full on. She looked for signs of a joke and there were none.

"Do you know, Akanksha?"

"No. I don't think so. It's just that you look like someone I used to know. I wanted to see you closer, because the resemblance is striking. But I do not know an Akanksha."

At exactly nine o'clock, Pritham Da and Boudi arrived at Shika's hotel room, a phone call from reception announcing their arrival. Punctual and efficient, her cousin remained an exception to the Calcutta rule.

They surmised that it would be half an hour across the city, at the most, at this time in the morning and that they should leave now to make the most of the late Calcutta starts. This time they sat in Pritham Da's car, a five-year-old silver Honda City. They had the luxury of closed windows and air conditioning, and the ride was smooth and seats comfortable. Shika was glad of the reprieve today from the jaundiced Ambies, as they were affectionately known. Her eyes darted from the chaos of the life outside to the serenity and quiet they had in the car. She wondered how people stayed here all their lives. Why wasn't there a daily uprising at the struggle of so many? Pritham Da talked about the city, telling her things had improved greatly. Shika was glad of the distraction, of the conversations that were not about the woman she was on her way to meet.

Suddenly wondering if she should have taken a gift with her, she asked her cousin's opinion and he looked to his wife to deliver her verdict, and they stopped at a chocolate shop on the corner of Park Street. A few white faces sat eating what looked like bacon and eggs, a few brown faces gesticulated as if they were lecturing. Shika looked at the chocolates and pastries behind the glass and unexpectedly felt transported back to a past that refused to be exorcised. She felt claustrophobic, in need of the present, her own reality. Hurriedly she selected a variety of chocolates and truffles.

Back in the car, they passed buildings with wooden frames with ornate fretwork, carved lattices and painted shutters, making Shika think of palaces and Sleeping Beauty; everything looked as it had twenty years ago when she was here for her wedding. The thought that she had been married for twenty years already was staggering. How much had she changed in those years in comparison to the city? They passed the zoo, the Victoria Memorial. She saw some more white people, this time on a horse drawn carriage, as they exclaimed and wondered at the grandeur of the Raj.

Shika pictured Akanksha walking through one of these scenes seen through the glass. She did not want to think of the girl child who grew up knowing her father had left her. She saw her smiling, hand in hand with someone she often looked up at; she imagined her to be happy now, with children of her own.

They drove through alleyways and side roads where toddlers were being bathed on pavements next to the nearest tube well. There were food stalls where giant aluminium pots bubbled and steamed on stoves. A rickety table and bench would seat one, maybe two customers at a time to take their morning meal before starting work.

Pritham Da's car continued until it finally stopped in front of some wrought iron gates. The building was painted green, a shade lighter than the green baize of a billiards table. The front door was wooden, with an ornate knocker and plastic doorbell next to the frame.

Flanked by her cousin and Boudi on either side, Shika tried the bell. There was no response for some time. She knocked on the door, creaking the knocker up and slamming down hard, twice, three times. This time the door opened. An old woman, Shika guessed to be a maid looked inquiringly at them, and Shika asked whether Akanksha Mukherjee lived there. The maid asked them to wait while she fetched her mistress. A few minutes later an older woman arrived. Her hair was thinning and a dirty, oily grey, and her sari was an almond-coloured silk. The sindoor on her forehead was smudged and her spectacles perched on her nose were wire rimmed and almost invisible.

"Who are you? What do you want?"

"I'm a relative of Akanksha's. I live in the U.K. I was hoping to meet her."

"How wonderful, come in." The old woman seemed genuinely pleased. Shika felt a wave of relief.

She was led into a room painted the same shade of green as the outside of the house, with beautifully carved rosewood furniture. Artificial flowers stood in vases, collecting dust; crocheted doilies covered the electrical appliances; a VCR, a cable box and the television all stood in the corner, the latter a gigantic box with pictures dancing on the screen. Shika was reminded of her father, hunched over, repairing his own ancient televisions years ago. The old woman pressed a button on the remote control and the pictures stood still with a look of surprise planted on the characters' faces.

"Akanksha has never had relatives who have visited before. You must have been very close, although I do not remember you at the wedding."

Shika explained that she could not make the wedding as she was living abroad. She waited for the old woman to produce Akanksha, so she could see her, maybe speak to her, and then be on her way. But the old woman seemed in no hurry to move.

"My husband and I have just come back from our morning walk, so it is lucky we came back early, or we would have missed you. He's upstairs now, waiting for his tea. Let me call him down."

The old woman called for the maid and asked her to make tea for them all. She instructed her to fetch some vegetable chops and shingara from one of the stalls nearby and told her to arrange them all on plates with the sweetmeats. Her excited instructions made Shika feel like an inconvenience, and she felt somewhat of a fraud in the overflowing reception room, pretending she was here for pleasant chit-chat with a much beloved relative.

Akanksha's mother-in-law excused herself whilst she went upstairs to fetch her husband, leaving them alone for some time. They looked at each other quizzically until Boudi asked what they all were thinking.

"Where's Akanksha?"

They waited for what seemed like a long time before an

old man clad in a snow-white dhoti and shirt appeared. He was completely bald except for patches of white just above his ears. His eyes, bluish grey with cataracts, peered through wire rimmed spectacles similar to his wife's and his hands shook as he held them out to guests.

"I must apologise for my wife," he began.

The front door slammed shut and the old woman's voice could be heard shrieking at the maid for being so wasteful. There was no reply from the maid.

"She should have told you that Akanksha does not stay with us any longer. She left many, many years ago. 1981 or '82, I think."

"Did they go somewhere in India or did they travel abroad?"

"Sorry. Let me explain." Mr Mukherjee pressed the top of his nose with this thumb and forefinger. He removed his spectacles and placed them in his shirt pocket. He paused before continuing, speaking slowly as if Shika and her cousins would have difficulty understanding. "My son and Akanksha divorced earlier that year. She left and we have not heard from her since then. My wife was devastated by the whole affair and sometimes forgets that Akanksha is not with us any longer. I believe she genuinely thought she might be able to produce her for you. She's been getting confused lately. The doctors are saying that it's Alzheimer's."

Shika's face fell. She was disappointed but there were other emotions she could not name playing inside her. She thanked the old man and got up to leave. Pritham Da and

Boudi were already by the front door. They put their shoes back on, awkwardly balancing as they slotted their bare feet into their sandals.

In the car, no one spoke. Shika noticed the box of chocolates she had forgotten to take inside with her. She offered them to Boudi who opened the box and took one; Shika took one too, disappointed again that it did not match the taste of the chocolate she was accustomed to. She remembered this same feeling when she tried chocolate in Calcutta the last time she was here. Nothing had changed. After a while it seemed like the logical conclusion was for Akanksha to be just a name without a face; Shika led a life a million miles away from Calcutta; She had met Akanksha's mother and that should have been enough.

Pritham Da and Boudi decided they needed to have drink. The car eventually turned right into a leafy entrance where a security guard handed their driver a token. Along a gravel path it went, stopping outside a group of bamboo tables and chairs. They all got out of the car which was driven off into some unknown direction. They would sit in the sun, they decided, under a giant red parasol with more gravel underfoot.

They looked out onto a huge expanse of green, rolling waves of neatly manicured grass. Shika had not seen so much space in Calcutta before. A waiter in a white and green uniform, with hair oiled neatly into a side parting, magically appeared and served them water in neat cylindrical glasses. Shika hesitated before Pritham Da assured her it was safe. They ordered wine, which quickly went to Shika's head. She felt lighter now, like a helium balloon accidentally released, untethered and slightly lost, but above and out of the mess.

She picked at the snacks her cousin ordered and wondered why she had not found this fresh air earlier. They chatted without saying much, whilst Pritham Da tried to educate her on the history of where they were. A Moghul king's family featured somewhere in the story and Shika tried to remain interested, but she could not retain the facts being related and eventually she was forced to hold up her hands to ask Pritham Da to stop. She saw some more mynah birds pecking at the crumbs left by other guests and realised that they really were everywhere. Her brain wandered, taking turns and wrong turns. She was not sure how lucid she sounded when she replied to questions or statements that were directed at her.

She walked to the ladies' room, passing sleeping dogs, letting them lie, afraid of their reaction if she got too close, passing jasmine blossoms that looked like white stars against the dark green foliage. She stopped to pick one and tried to catch the scent, but was disappointed when she could smell nothing. Women, some wearing cycling shorts and tennis shoes and some wearing elegant saris, stopped to glance at Shika. She stared back at them, daring them to challenge her with more than just disdain in their eyes, but they were smiling. There was no malice, just curiosity. Shika was forced to smile back.

19

"I'll love you always, you know!"

"I know."

"When I die, I'll come back as a ghost and watch over you!"

"That's a little creepy."

They fell apart laughing, then, lying in each other's arms in a field of poppies by the side of the road.

The memory was like a painting. A couple in the long grass, surrounded by wildflowers, insects buzzing innocuously, a song playing from the car radio like a soundtrack to the whole event, the clouds making ivory horses and downy hearts in a cerulean sky.

It was still fresh in Shika's mind. It was the first month after she had married her husband. Speaking of death was a joke then, but today, it held a different significance. Too much had happened: she had learnt that no one was immune to death, that it could come to anyone, at any moment. She had learnt that reality was not always what she perceived it to be and truth was malleable, like a clay pot before it is dried.

She watched Tara as she slept. She still had the look of the child she remembered. Her eyelids fluttered as if she was dreaming and Shika did not want to think about what her daughter had gone through while she was away.

She had found the leaflet accidentally in her rucksack as she was cleaning it out. There would be no scarring that could be seen after what Tara had done. Scars came after giving birth. But she would not forget. Shika would remember what her child had done every time she looked at her. She was not sure what it was that angered her the most, whether it was that her daughter had chosen to wipe out an innocent life or whether it was that she had taken part in the act to create life in the first place. She wondered what her husband would say, no doubt he would be equally devastated, if not more. Tara was his little girl.

When Tara was about two years old she would refuse her mother feeding her or bathing her, and would stubbornly wait for her father to return from work. They would sit together on Tara's bed, under the covers with a torch, making up stories about talking clouds and a Magic Man and they would giggle and scream until Shika would worry that Tara would not be able to settle to sleep. Shika would try to think of stories from the top of her head, but it never worked. Tara instead would pick out a book and ask Shika to read it to her.

They would sit upright on the covers, rather than under them, and Tara was easily irritated with any mistake Shika made. All mistakes were forgiven though for her father.

Shika had the same relationship with her own father. She knew what it was to ache with longing when her Baba would return late from an errand or from work. She was angry at her mother when she left, but it was not the same. She wondered if her mother felt jealous of her relationship with her father, the way sometimes Shika felt jealous of her husband and Tara.

Shika went back downstairs. The kitchen was cold. She shivered constantly since returning from Calcutta, even though the thermostat was turned up. She made herself a cup of tea and turned on the television. She could not sleep. She wondered if her life would have turned out differently if Ambika had made the same choice as Tara. Shika had no knowledge of the man who made her daughter pregnant and felt no desire to, but a part of her wanted to be reassured that no lives were destroyed by their actions.

She considered confronting Tara in the morning with what she had learned and then decided against. It was not her place any more to tell Tara what to do, her daughter was a grown woman who made her own decisions. A part of Shika even felt proud. Her daughter would not be lost or in need of a hand to hold at every turn.

20

When Tara was very small, about five or six years old, she begged her parents for a pet. Her father almost relented but Shika objected vehemently. They were struggling to feed themselves, she said, how were they expected to take care of another creature?

A pet would love her, a pet would take care of her, like Lassie did for her owner, Tara thought. Being an early reader, Tara had discovered the Worst Witch books and like Mildred Hubble she dreamed of owning a cat.

On one of the days when Shika could barely get out of bed, Tara felt a deep and unsettling urge to run away, to escape. It had been a troublesome week, with both of her parents emotionally absent and impatient. Her mother's deep low sobs kept Tara awake and her desire to escape had become overpowering.

There was no pre-planning, no packing of a suitcase and no note explaining her grief. Instead, Tara wore only her dressing gown over her pink nighty covered in pictures of cats and quietly, in her fluffy bat slippers, slipped out into the cool summer night.

Exhilaration soon turned to panic as everything familiar now looked sinister and odd. Sounds she had heard a million times from the confines of the walls of her house, or as she held her parents' hands, now seemed louder. Tara spun around where she stood just a few steps from her own front gate and could not make up her mind whether to go back inside or run. She decided to run, fearing her father's disappointment and her mother's fury when they found out what Tara had attempted to do. She broke into a sprint and ran along the street, not daring to cross over, despite the lack of cars driving past. She stopped, breathless, when she reached the crossroad. Exhausted and lonely, she fell to the floor, the tiny grey stones from the cracked pavement, digging into her knees and her palms, where she leant. As she sobbed, a gentle mewing joined her. A little furry head nudged at the crook of her elbow, tiny teeth tugged at her dressing gown, softly biting down, not hard enough to break skin, but painful enough to get Tara's full attention finally.

Tara carried the little thing all the way home. concocting a fantastical story about how she heard the kitten mewling outside and had to see what it was. They would believe her, she was sure, preferring that story over the alternative that Tara had attempted to run away. She rang the bell, slightly nervous, but deeply happy all the same. The warmth of the kitten in her arms, the way his rough tongue tickled her fingers, occasionally biting, as if to remind her to keep petting, filled her up like nothing else had.

Her father opened the door. He looked at his daughter. He did not see the kitten at first. The story rushed out of Tara's mouth before her father could ask any questions, leaving him speechless.

Shika appeared behind her husband, secretly watching and listening.

"Tell her she can keep the kitten until we find it a new home." Shika's verdict was final. She went into kitchen to make up some milk for the baby and Tara almost cried with joy and relief.

That night she slept with the kitten in her bed, both curled up and content. Shika was too tired to protest and Mark was too resigned to the wills of his daughter and wife to object. He watched as his family slept for a while that night, then finally retired to bed himself, smiling as he closed his eyes.

The following morning Tara was awoken by a tiny paw tugging at her hair, chewing it, pulling it. She opened her eyes and realised she had not dreamed last night's events. She examined the creature that had found her, and watched in wonder as his pupils dilated and contracted. She looked at his beautiful grey fur, laced with black patches that sometimes seemed like the spots of a cheetah. She revelled in the softness of his belly; she saw the depth of his ears, deep as caves, as pink as coral and knew she only had to whisper for her little one to hear her. She whispered, "I love you," and he seemed to reply, "and I, you,".

She ran around looking for things to make her kitten's life

easier. It did not occur to her to worry that her mother did not kiss her good morning or that her father did not hug her goodbye as he left for the shops. Her priority was Nibbles. Shika, annoyed at first, but then relieved to see her daughter distracted and busy, helped. She set out two bowls for the kitten, one for food and one for water. She fed it scraps from the night before and was as relieved as Tara when the food bowl was licked clean. They let it out in the garden to dig, play and chase and Shika was glad she had not planted anything yet. They talked about finding a vet and secretly Shika worried about the costs, but she did not mention that to her happy daughter. Thoughts of running away did not occur to Tara after that.

A few months later Nibbles was let out as usual and had found a gap in the fence. He crawled through and never came back.

Tara never kept a pet after that, but searched instead for that love elsewhere, and was unsurprised that it did not appear.

Tara remembered her aunt's funeral and the lack of colour that day. The clouds were white, everyone was wearing white, including herself, and her mother's hand as she held it, was white. She remembered watching her mother cry and her grandmother being comforted by one of the other old Bengali ladies. She had just had her hair cut short and felt self-conscious. She remembered admiring a younger cousin's dress, white with butterflies embroidered all the way through. She remembered wondering how she would feel if it was her mother lying in the coffin. Her aunt looked asleep. Someone had washed and dressed her, and she looked beautiful. She wondered why she couldn't cry like everyone else – was there something wrong with her? She did not want anyone to think she was strange, so she pretended to sob on her mother's shoulder as her mother held her and let her own tears fall in silence.

She wanted her father to be there, but he had decided not to come. He wanted Shika to mourn with her family, with her community. He and Aunty Bella never really knew each other, and Tara never really questioned why.

Tara looked at Aunty Bella again. She was not beautiful like her mother, but she was much more fun. She envied the way she used to wear fashionable clothes and loved the way she would tickle her whenever she came to visit, when Tara was younger and she was a much better cook. Tara had often wished that Aunty Bella was her mother.

Now, Aunty Bella was gone, so was Dadu, her grandfather. Her mother remained, unchanging, still the most beautiful woman she knew.

Tara looked back at herself and wanted to forgive all the silly petty mistakes she had made as a child, because they really were small compared to the ones she made as she grew up. She hugged herself and wondered if anyone would find her before she became cold. She supposed not. It did not matter anyway.

21

It was Shika who found her. Her emotions stopped, just long enough for her to bind her daughter's wrists with the scarves from her Indian suits. She rang the ambulance and waited. Her mother was taking her regular afternoon nap, and Shika did not wake her; she did not know what she would say. But she rang her husband and let it ring until she was asked to leave a message. She hung up. She rang the neighbour who let herself in with a key. Shika told her she just needed to be here for her mother when she woke up.

Shika watched her husband walk in just behind the paramedics. He could not look away and yet he could do nothing to help. He watched helplessly, arms by his side, fists clenched, as the paramedics checked for a pulse and bound her wrists properly. He had to be asked to move as they carried the gurney down.

Shika remembered listening as they told her that her

daughter would be fine. She still had a pulse. She was lucky she was found in time. Shika had only walked into Tara's room to finally confront her about the abortion. She would not have found her otherwise. She would have left her to her own devises as she had been instructed to do, time and time again.

They sat in the ambulance with her. They watched her as she slept, as she was rocked and jolted, her head wobbling helplessly like a corpse.

She realised she shook with rage, not fear. She wanted to slap her daughter hard across the face and see the shock in her eyes. When Shika went into labour with her first child, she did not know it. She remembered experiencing stomach cramps that she would normally attribute to indigestion. She remembered feeling as if she needed the toilet and if she could just have one decent bowel movement she would be fine. She remembered asking for Gaviscon to ease the pain and she remembered her mother stroking her back. It was her mother who told her she thought that the baby was coming. Her husband was telephoned and would meet them at the hospital. Chotu, who had long ago stopped being Chotu, would drive them there, as he was the only one with a car. His name was Amit, he reminded them time and time again. They debated whether to call an ambulance. Shika said she would wait for Chotu to arrive. When he finally did arrive, she knew she was in labour. The pains had become intense, making her double over. She felt as if she were being torn in four different directions and she wanted to cry. But the pain stopped from time to time and during those moments Shika believed that she would be able to do this.

The midwife was a Punjabi woman who had just retired and only came back on shift because they were short staffed. She told Shika and her mother that she would take no nonsense. She slapped Shika's legs and told her to stop pushing. Shika screamed at her, told her she couldn't help it. The midwife would slap her legs again and tell her to get over it.

Somehow Shika was able to deliver a healthy baby girl. Mark was called into the room and given the girl to hold. He asked Shika's mother's permission to name the girl after the daughter that she had lost. She had tears in her eyes as she assented. Tara locked eyes with her grandmother then, looking at her from her father's arms. Mamta would not hear that new born babies could not focus much farther than their face at that stage; Mamta swore that her own Tara looked back at her and gave her blessing to them all for being the family that they had become.

Mamta watched their next-door neighbour talking to her. She understood some words. She had heard the ambulance and the voices of the paramedics coming up the stairs and at first worried they had come for her. These days she worried every time she fell asleep whether she would wake up again. She soon realised that they were here for Tara. She did not know what had happened as she could not follow the English. Then she heard the word 'suicide' and knew what that meant. She could not move.

The neighbour pulled up a chair to Mamta's bed. She smelled of flowers and fried onions and talked in English while Mamta ignored her. She stayed in the room with Mamta until she convinced her that she would be fine. She helped her get out of bed and Mamta was able to make her way to Tara's room, as the neighbour went downstairs.

There were blood stains on Tara's carpet. Dark red drops which would be hard to remove, thought Mamta.

Downstairs, the front door softly closed. The old woman was alone now, with only her ghosts who often came out at night. Perhaps she would see her child again, the Tara who left this world when she was too young. She looked back into a misty dark, searching for the explanation of what she was experiencing, what they all were experiencing now.

She prayed because that was all she knew.

⁘

Shika read the words on her phone in the hospital waiting room. She was trying to make sense of what had just happened. She did not understand why Tara would think that dying would be better than living. After everything she thought they had given her, it did not make sense. She felt she had failed as her mother, for not being able to protect her, and wondered if it was the abortion, the shame, the guilt – or the loss which forced her daughter to make such a choice. Some part of her wanted to blame herself for her melancholy early on. Was it inherited? She had always feared it, looking for signs in Tara throughout her life, waiting for it to surface. Were the books she read, the friends she kept, the factors which convinced her that death was an answer? Was she smoking or taking drugs? There was a darkness, as far as her daughter's life was concerned; a corner that would never be lit up. She asked her questions into the darkness, but the darkness remained silent.

Shika watched her husband as he rocked back and forth, hands clasped to his chin. His eyes were fixed on his daughter as if to will her awake. Shika stepped over the threshold of the room and touched his shoulder. He did not look at Shika as he rose; he did not say anything. Perhaps he blamed her, she thought.

It was her turn to watch, wait, and will the girl awake. What would she say to her when she did? There were no words. The tears came now; hot and unrelenting. They bubbled and boiled over like hot milk. Shika was helpless. And then there was nothing.

Tara looked peaceful now. She wanted her to stay asleep for a hundred years, like Sleeping Beauty. She had never really known how to handle her. It was Mark who would manage the tantrums and demands, distracting her, telling her stories, convincing her that they were proud of her, that they knew she would always do the right thing. Shika wanted to tell her now that they still loved her, were still proud of her because she knew when Tara would wake up she would feel a failure; she could not be perfect, could not make the right decision this time. Her guilt would lie in their pain and Shika knew that she did not possess the strength to convince her daughter otherwise.

Tara's eyelids began to flutter. She was waking. She tried to speak. Shika began to stand to leave the room but felt her daughter's hand on her wrist. She sat down again, giving in, but was not yet able to look at the girl who had just opened her eyes.

Burra Bazaar was quiet at this time of day. Anjana felt unhurried and decided to browse a little through the stalls before she finally made her way home to her bed. The stall keepers did not encourage her, yet they did not shoo her away; it was quiet enough for them not worry about a hijra's presence until the evening, when their more serious customers would arrive. They slumped against their walls on their stools and watched Anjana lazily through half closed eyes as she fingered their goods and walked on.

She looked at the gaudy wind-up and inflatable toys and cheap plastic wares out on display. She glanced at the t-shirts and jeans designed for sixteen-year olds who wanted to look like they belonged in America. Then she stopped at the bangle seller. Every colour Anjana could hope for was out on display. She picked up the perfect circles of glass or metal, grouped in fours, sixes or eights, examined them and looked for the price. She put them down. She was in no mood to haggle. Today, she wanted to be quiet. She was used up

Overhead, green and silver flags glittered on lines ready for the celebration of Eid. They criss-crossed and fluttered and caught the sun, reminding Anjana of all those years ago when she had been found and taken in. It must have been this time of year: the flags were out then too, she remembered the call to prayer, the smells of food, the goats tired and restless

Somewhere in her mind the image of a woman kneeling, her head covered, eyes closed and praying, drifted and settled. Her palms were open, outstretched as if receiving a gift and her lips moved in silent prayer. Anjana knew the words, for she had already been taught to speak them when she could barely speak, taught to turn her head and kneel just so. But that was before she became Anjana. She remembered what Akanksha had said before she stepped onto the bus, and prayed for her now, wondering who she was today.

A few minutes later, Anjana found herself outside the pet store. There was a small cage of about six baby rabbits, balls of grey and white fluff, tumbling over each other. There were more cages of birds: parakeets, lovebirds, even a bright green parrot. As she walked inside, she could see glass bowls and aquariums filled with goldfish and Siamese fighter fish. And then she heard the strangest voice.

"Durgaa, Durga!" it called.

She noticed a big black cage on the other side of the stall, away from the other birds. The owner was dozing in the early afternoon heat, but the bird was awake and alert.

"Durgaa, Durga," it repeated.

Anjana stared. In all of her years she had never heard a bird speak, had only heard tales of it occurring. She moved closer and examined its eyes. It looked straight at her as if it were examining her too. The dark brown, dowdy wings and the gold around its eyes made it seem a painted misfit, much like herself.

"How much?" she asked the stall keeper.

"Too much for you!" he responded, irritated at being disturbed. He closed his eyes again and ignored her.

She examined the cage once more and silently pulled out

the pin holding the cage door closed. The bird watched, fascinated, cocking its head to one side. It walked sideways across the bar it was on and the cage clattered a little where it hung. The door opened just a touch and Anjana walked home, willing herself not to look back.

Ya devi sarva bhuteshu, shanti rupena sangsthita Ya devi sarva bhuteshu, shakti rupena sangsthita
Ya devi sarva bhuteshu, matri rupena sangsthita Yaa devi sarva bhuteshu, buddhi rupena sangsthita Namastasyai, namastasyai, namastasyai, namo namaha

'The goddess who is omnipresent as the personification of the universal mother The goddess who is omnipresent as the embodiment of power The goddess who is omnipresent as the symbol of peace Oh Goddess (Devi) who resides everywhere in all living beings as intelligence and beauty, I bow to her, I bow to her, I bow to her again & again.'

Acknowledgements

I would like to thank my editors, Robert Peett, Tia Albert, Izzy Cash and Rabia Butt for helping to transform this novella into something polished and worthy of being read. Without the Novella Project and Holland House, I think I would still be dreaming instead of doing.

Thank you to my husband who knew I needed to write from the very start of everything. Words, ironically, fall short of expressing my gratitude to him, for the time and space to write and his patience when I finally decided that this was what I was going to do. Thank you to my children, who believe in me as much as I believe in them.

I thank my friends, and family because I never thank them enough for nurturing my love of books and stories, for reading my writing and for sharing their opinions, Nisha in particular, who simply but overwhelmingly, took the time to be there through it all.

And finally, thank you to Kolkata and the works of Tagore; without the City of Joy and a well-worn collection of short stories, there would be no Akanksha, no Anjana, no Tinku and no Saira.

About the Author

Devjani Bodepudi was born into Bengali home in the mountains of North East India. She came to England when she was just a year old because this was where her mother called home.

Once she had graduated from University, Devjani trained to be a Primary school teacher, where she hoped to nurture her love of reading in those she taught.

After falling in love, a story in itself, and having two children, Devjani and her family moved to Kolkata which led her to a dream job of working as an Editor for Kindle Mag where she published several short stories, poems, articles and interviews.

Devjani is now back in the UK, working as a teacher and writing her second novel.